PAVEL LEMBERSKY

# THE DEATH OF SAMUSIS, AND OTHER STORIES

BOSTON • 2020

**Pavel Lembersky**

The Death of Samusis, and Other Stories

ISBN 978-1950319305

Library of Congress Control Number: 2020945440

Book Layout by Yulia Tymoshenko
Author Photograph by Anatoli Stepanenko
Cover Design by Elif Mete
Cover Art ("Procession of Monsters") by Suzan Batu
Cover Photograph by Al Lapkovsky

PUBLISHED BY M·GRAPHICS | BOSTON, MA

www.mgraphics-publishing.com
mgraphics.books@gmail.com

Printed in the United States of America

Acknowledgment is made to the following publications in which some of the stories in this book have originally appeared: "Humble Beginnings", "So Long, Dos Passos", "Status Quo" in *Little Star Journal;* "The Lost Bet" in *Habitus magazine;* "2 Sisters", "The Last Words", "Nothing but Tights" in *Calque magazine;* "Snoopy Goes to Kasimov" in *Words Without Borders;* "Visiting the Girlfriends" in *Fiction International;* "Tony + Lyuda = Love" in *Gobshite;* "The Dead Wave" in *Fustercluck;* "Wish You Were Here: A Few Postcards from New York" in *The Brooklyn Rail;* "The Death of Samusis" in *Trafika Europe;* Cat-Dogs in *Gargoyle.*

The talented Pavel Lembersky, Jewish Odessan heritage pulsing in his literary arteries, adroitly talks the Russian expat talk as he walks the American immigrant walk. Lembersky's verbal art is nothing short of a wonder. Once a Soviet teenager quickly outfitted to write original American prose, Lembersky has steadfastly followed the example of the leading lights of early Russian émigré literature—Aldanov, Berberova, Gazdanov—by refusing to trade in his Russian quill pen even after decades of living in America. *The Death of Samusis* generously showcases Lembersky's achievement as a writer of shorter fiction—a fearless chronicler of exile, a loving absurdist of desire, a paradoxist of life's endless bifurcation.

— Maxim D. Shrayer,
Boston College professor
and author of *A Russian Immigrant*

# Content

Humble Beginnings . . . . . . . . . . . . . . . . . . . . . . 11

So Long, Dos Passos . . . . . . . . . . . . . . . . . . . . . 12

The Lost Bet . . . . . . . . . . . . . . . . . . . . . . . . . . 16

Sax Solo . . . . . . . . . . . . . . . . . . . . . . . . . . . . . 20

The Foreskin . . . . . . . . . . . . . . . . . . . . . . . . . . 25

2 Sisters . . . . . . . . . . . . . . . . . . . . . . . . . . . . . 37

Snoopy Goes to Kasimov . . . . . . . . . . . . . . . . . . 42

Among the Stones . . . . . . . . . . . . . . . . . . . . . . . 49

Oleg, Mila, and I, and Honolulu, and the Korean . . . . . . 52

Visiting the Girlfriends . . . . . . . . . . . . . . . . . . . 55

Tony + Lyuda = Love . . . . . . . . . . . . . . . . . . . . . 57

The Dead Wave . . . . . . . . . . . . . . . . . . . . . . . . . 60

Status Quo . . . . . . . . . . . . . . . . . . . . . . . . . . . . 63

Wish You Were Here: A Few Postcards from New York . . . 66

Bobby the Loon . . . . . . . . . . . . . . . . . . . . . . . . . 73

some folks call it paranoia . . . . . . . . . . . . . . . . . 80

De Kooning . . . . . . . . . . . . . . . . . . . . . . . . . . . 83

The Death of Samusis . . . . . . . . . . . . . . . . . . . . . 88

Chronicle of a Murder . . . . . . . . . . . . . . . . . . . . 95

Five Easy Pieces . . . . . . . . . . . . . . . . . . . . . . . 102

The '90s . . . . . . . . . . . . . . . . . . . . . . . . . . . . . 113

Love Gone South . . . . . . . . . . . . . . . . . . . . . . . 122

Rehearsal . . . . . . . . . . . . . . . . . . . . . . . . . . . . 129

The Last Words . . . . . . . . . . . . . . . . . . . . . . . . 136

Nothing but Tights . . . . . . . . . . . . . . . . . . . . . . 140

Once in a Lifetime . . . . . . . . . . . . . . . . . . . . . . 145

Cat–Dogs . . . . . . . . . . . . . . . . . . . . . . . . . . . . 159

# Humble Beginnings

I was born and raised, you will recall if you peruse the society pages with any degree of regularity, in my maternal grandfather's log house in the fair town of Kislodrotsk. Humble beginnings, you might call my formative years. I call it child abuse. 100 pushups with koromyslo, no ifs or buts, prodrazverstka with DA, lend-lease, anybody? You bet your bottom Stradivarius. Times were rough (but are they ever not?), collectivization to give you one glaring example of polysyllabic madness, no sense of history, who is Liubov Orlova the benumbed ipod kids of today ask and scratch their bazookas in faux bewilderment. Whatever. They run on gastric juices alone, they have no shame to speak of. But neither did Tatiana and I. So please, no mudslinging while I wallow in nostalgia and gasp for oxygen, tovarichi.

# So Long, Dos Passos

It's just that long long ago we lived in a city by the sea where in the summertime our bodies tanned brown as chocolate. We started smoking early and in July we would entertain ourselves by flipping our cigarette butts off the balcony and making bets on whether they'd land on the sidewalk or hang suspended in the leaves of the chestnut trees, swaying. The smoke from the cheap cigarettes clenched in the corners of our mouths made us squint as we played popular tunes on our guitars. At dusk we would stroll out with our lady loves. We were envied. No wonder—we were young, with bell-bottoms and bad English, we laughed with exaggerated gaiety. Granted, the Beatles had split up. Well, so what. So the Beatles split up. Her eyes were still like deep dark pools, you could drown in them.

And watching the sun come up on the boulevard? Cool kvass on hot humid nights? Not another soul on the square. We sit at the foot of the monument and read your beloved Mann. Aloud. Thomas, Thomas. We love theatrical gestures, especially on public transportation:

"Citizens, your tickets please?"

"I've got a free pass."

Then the whole bus joins the chase, like in that Breughel, the reproduction at our dacha that winter, no parents and no electricity, the three of us drinking mulled wine out of a shared glass in the dark. We're young, you know? Just tell me one thing. Where does it all go, leaving you nothing but heartburn? Where to? Into the sand? Through your fingers? Tell me.

Hey Jude? Sang it. Sang them all. Seems like the Beatles were all we had. But now we didn't even have them.

Your first date? Let me remind you: you—hooked nose, bedroom eyes, sensitive lips, chestnut-brown hair, corduroy jacket with threadbare elbows. Overcoat—duffel. You wait for her on the corner by the candy store. She's innocence itself, a breath of air, a white-tailed fawn... those eyes, those eyes! Shy movements, awkward jokes, too late for the movies, too early for home, short on cash for cafes but try one kiss and it's "I'll call the police." Her relatives still an unknown—but as for you, well, papa's a doctor, mama's a doctor, grandpa's a doctor, grandma's dead, but she was a doctor too, first rank. The profession's in your blood, fine by you, all the Trachtenbergs are dermatologists. But she's from out of town, hasn't been here long, talks a little oddly, makes writing mistakes and my god can you believe she's never read Feuchtwanger? Not wagner, wanger. The Jewish War? That's about aggression in the Middle East, right? Jud Süss? We've got a tailor named Zuss in our building. Senya. Senya Zuss.

And then there's another twist: her secret admirer, the son of someone in the Security Organs, he's aiming for the same kind of job, Mr. Designer-Label—platforms, Levi's, right jacket, right dope, *Machine Head*, daddy's Grundig—and he's kicking himself right now and hoping to put our Romeo away for a long long time with no mail privileges, but it just so happens you prefer the epistolary genre, and she just loves your epistles. See, you've got this romance-by-mail thanks to a certain carrier pigeon with a broken wing (I was in a cast for two months, fell off my bicycle) but you couldn't send anything to her address—her father was a real hard-ass. And you were in school somewhere else, they were asking three thousand to get into the med institute here and your uncle (also a doctor, but an ear-nose-throat man) could only scrape up fifteen hundred, and all fifteen hundred would get you was construction engineering and you hate construction, you start twitching at the very words "directional angle," you want to cure disease or if worse comes to worst study languages—read Faulkner without a dictionary, Dos Passos in the original, Ford Madox Ford like the back of your hand. And that's how it eventually worked out—fifteen hundred gets you the foreign language institute, but in Rostov instead of here. Meanwhile there you are at the candy store, you take her hand and raise it to your lips to warm it up, and she laughs, she's embarrassed but grateful.

But her secret admirer ratted you out, and then sicced his pals on you besides, because Security Organs are all well and good, but a good ass-stomping, excuse the prosaic expression, never hurt anyone either. A preemptive strike. In a word—bloody nose, bloody coat, she's in tears, you're in a snowbank. She helps you get up, you lean on her skinny elbow, try to crack a joke, but somehow you're missing the teeth for it. That's how your romance began. What came next? As far as I can recall—the four seasons.

Wintertime—you're a bit ironic. Three weeks passed. It was the end of February. Another snowbank, with a bathhouse whisk in it. The neighbor lady complained: I've got blood pressure, and they're not heating the place. You didn't see each other much, and when you did you fought. I tried to avoid you together. I watched you from behind a kiosk, through tears. You would kiss, multiply, kiss. Once I was standing on the corner by the candy store; she came up from behind and put her hands over my eyes. I could guess who it was from the smell. Her hands smelled of your tobacco. She was surprised. "How could you tell?" I made some lame joke. She was in a hurry to get to class. Her Polish boots squeaked on the snow. I wonder, if I'd told her how I felt back then, how would things have turned out? Just the same, or not?

Springtime—a bit romantic. Tan raincoat, sideburns, she's got a chignon. She pinches your earlobe, you quote Nadson, I pretend I'm absorbed in the movie on TV. *The Irony of Fate* or *No Right to Be Oneself*, I can't remember. You got nicknamed Stroker, because all you did was stroke her head, supposedly. Turned out you did a little more than that. You also tickled her nipples with your tongue, and her calves would go all goosebumpy. Her father taught thermodynamics, her mother did too. She's thirty-six now, the boy's about to turn ten. They say her looks are ruined, she's gained weight. I don't know, to me she looks the same as she always did.

Autumn—melancholic. What else? Secret admirer's daddy put your uncle away on a bribery count, you got kicked out of your institute, so did the dean. So long, Dos Passos. Hello construction detail. But you hated construction as much as ever, and so you decided to apply for an exit visa, and you started getting ready, little by little. You promised to come back and get her, but you didn't come back, and you didn't get her, and instead you grew a beard and bought a house with a nice lawn and started selling computers somewhere around Cincinnati. At first she cried every night, then she got over it and married her secret admirer, who had, by the time you left, finally come in from the cold. He brings home flowers every evening. Must mean he loves her. Must mean even Security Organs are capable of real emotion. . .

I open the door, there she is in her washed-out housecoat, smoking L&M's, grumbling, "Glads again, what a surprise"; out on the balcony our son is playing with the collie. I thank my lucky stars. She was and is everything I ever wanted or needed. From anything or anyone.

We hardly ever think about you. There's not much reason to. Except in the summertime. That summer you were so strange. You kept staring at me, saying "Why do you hate me?" I'd get mad: "Are you crazy in the head or what?" You'd laugh this theatrical laugh, I'd shrug, make circles with my index finger around my temple, you'd slap me on the back and say, declarative, interrogative, I don't know, "M'boy, you just don't get the joke. . ."

*translated by Jane Miller*

# The Lost Bet

Finally we heard the shot. Collin had shot himself. There was a general sigh of relief. The night was still young. Next up a toast for the coming year 199. . . Greg, surfer boy from California, had already managed to get on the general nerves with his camera. He was in New York for five days; when somebody told him that Collin and I had a bet—$10,000 he blows his brains out on New Year's—Greg decided to ditch his relatives in Bay Ridge and showed up instead at our place. In case I lost the ten grand were to be paid out to Collin's sister Oona. Oona was spending the evening with Greg's relatives in Bay Ridge. She worked at a women's boutique in Soho, somewhere like Mercer St. She knew nothing of the bet.

Only a handful of the guests knew about it too (Stacy didn't have a clue): Rodger and his new wife from Mass., my nephew from Queens—his parents had dropped him off at our place and flew off to Paris—Greg, obviously, and that's it. I had been to Paris six years earlier, also around New Year's, and so I agreed to make my brother a list—fairly sizable, as it turned out—of must-sees and sound advice: like what to do when it rains or snows (Answer: pick a spot in a café, watch people. What could be better? Stacy doesn't agree with me, though: according to her there's nothing sweeter on a rainy day than the Musée d'Orsay. She's pretty obsessed with the 19th c. in general, though—you can leave her on a desert island with several oils of Delacroix and Courbet and she wouldn't know the difference.)

Greg had invited us out to California for the last New Year's: he's finishing up law school out there; in his free time (how is this jurist-in-the making finding free time, I'm thinking) he's running around San Francisco with his semipro camcorder, shooting anything he can get his lens on: tourist-packed cable cars, the bums on Market, the lesbian parade, the festival in Chinatown, etc. We got to see all of it that New Year's Eve, with a detailed commentary track. At first I was interested, then uninterested, then I started falling asleep. Stacy kept nudging me in the right side and querying Greg in a loud voice: How often do you have these parades? or Your bums really seem livelier than ours in New York, don't they?

Now I know that this was Stacy's way of making sure I didn't fall asleep completely and thereby mortally offend Greg. She's a kind, sensitive person, that Stacy.

The New Year's we ended up spending with his artist friends in Monterey. The party had a distinctly conceptualist tinge: instead of a tree there was a stump in the bedroom with two branches. One had a green ball, the other had a red ball. Everyone got hella stoned and got down to REM, then Run DMC, and LL Cool J. One of the high moments was Stacy dropping to her knees and yelling: "Clear the intersection, now! I'm talking to you!" Turned out she had briefly mistaken the tree for a traffic light, sans yellow. Past midnight we were joined by the neighbors: they were wearing black leather and had handcuffs protruding from their back pockets. There were no more than three of them, but somehow they managed to populate the entire house. Toward the very end I remember punching one of them in the face, then driving Greg's deformed Chevy home with one hand—the other was neatly packaged in ice. Greg was rather voluble (coke plus "ecstasy" I'm guessing); Stacy was sucking her thumb peacefully in the back.

"Just keep it in mind, Al—you're way stoned," contributed Greg to the non-existent conversation. "Don't drive too fast, but not too slow, either. The main thing is to try to avoid the cops."

"Why would I want to do that?"

"That's very funny, really, but this isn't the time to be funny, Al. Just listen to what I'm telling you: if you get pulled over don't start up with any kind of arguments. Think back to the worst possible fuck-up from your high school, the one they eventually kicked out for too much ass-kicking. That's the type that ends up on the force. I know those guys, trust me."

Driving down unfamiliar roads at three in the morning—stoned, one-handed, with Greg's blabber on the stereo—was no easy task. All things being equal, two hands would have been better.

Why did I punch out one of the leather-clad neighbors, I remember thinking the next morning in our temporary marital foldout. Finally I remembered: it seems he was trying to chat up Stacy.

"He's not interested in your Stacy," Greg lectured me over breakfast. "He's been married for almost a year now to the kid that came with him. Jealousy will be the ruin of you sooner or later. Mark my words, Al: ruin, end. Did you say coffee or tea?"

Greg had been seeing Collin's sister Oona for something like three years. Every now and then he called me up in New York to ask how things were going generally. "Come and see for yourself," I said, but he would get annoyed, and I had to appease him:

"She's working, daughter started school," I would say, though I'd see Oona about once a month at best and my information was probably old news to Greg.

How do people do this long-distance thing? She goes over once or twice a year, he comes out once or twice a year—but that's it, isn't it? As far as I knew she had no plans to move to California. His moving out here before getting his degree was out of the question. And then, what if he can't find work here? A life together is a never-ending compromise—I got to figure this one out a while ago. Stacy and I—well, we've managed to file down the rough edges a bit, learned to understand one another, I guess. Take me, for example—I'm not ready to have kids, and she isn't rushing me. On the other hand, she's been trying to get Collin to visit from New Zealand for a second year straight now—I say gladly, plenty of room, too.

Greg was just finishing setting up his tripod when Stacy went out into the hallway to usher in newly arriving friends. Greg had hooked up two additional spotlamps to his camcorder: one of them was clamped to the back of a chair, the other he handed to me and asked to keep it pointed at Collin. Then he switched on the camera and said to no one, "So. What's next?"

Collin had put on an embarrassed smile, I tried to keep calm, though I was ready—in case of forfeit—to dig into the ten grand with both hands. I was already going through the prospects: a decent stereo system? Down payment on a new car? A trip down somewhere like Indonesia or New Zealand—Collin, incidentally, has been trying to get us to come visit. Nothing wrong with Paris, don't get me wrong, but if that's all you ever get to see...

Collin drew a .45 pistol from his backpack and cocked the hammer.

"He's not kidding then," flashed through my mind, and I looked over at Greg, who was turning the zoom ring.

Collin hurriedly took the gun in his mouth and pulled the trigger. There was a noise. A red globule hit the wall just beside the cheap reproduction of Renoir's *Bathers* and immediately started on its way down. Collin fell to the floor.

"Let's hope that all the evils of the passing year depart, and the New Year brings us only joy," somebody said with overdone optimism, presumably Greg.

Where am I going to get the ten grand I owe Oona now—I don't even want to think about that.

*translated by Sergey Levchin*

# Sax Solo

This was no kind of mood; the worst kind. Tried reading. Nearly killed herself with *Madame Bovary*. Picked up *Mumu*—just about started howling. "Where is he already?" She was about to leave a note on the fridge "Put soup in microwave. I'm getting Samantha" when she heard the anxious rustle of his feet in the hallway. He was in high spirits, though. Five click pens tumbled out of his pocket, and he didn't even wait to take off his coat, but told her exactly how he had stayed after most of the staff had left for lunch and then tiptoed all the way to the secretary's desk and there—between the calendar and the telephone—he found the keys with a keychain like a Stop sign (didn't stop *me*, though, he laughed), and with keys pressed into his fist he went up to the cabinet (the one with the office supplies) and back again, and he did it three times to make sure that nobody was watching, and when the coast was clear he quickly picked out the one key—out of four—opened the cabinet door and swiped the pens.

"How's that?" he was looking at her, expecting—at the very least—a kiss to seal his triumph. She twisted her mouth to one side.

"What's with you?" he said, throwing his coat over the back of a chair en route to the refrigerator.

"Nothing," she said. She thought, "My husband is a clerk at an ad agency, he makes two hundred and twenty-five dollars a week, hates his job, steals pens from the cabinet to spite his boss, his fate, and ultimately himself."

"What's for dinner?" he said, pretending not to see her ill humor.

"Whatever you make," her voice came from the corridor.

Then he heard the door close: at six o'clock she went to pick up their daughter from practice.

No more than a year ago—no more—her eyes filled with quiet joy as she gazed into his sloping back before the window, where he stood silently, watching the snow land softly on the car roofs below.

"He isn't like the rest of them," she thought. "Right now something wonderful is happening inside that dear head."

Just one year! She collected his bons mots—even the flatter ones—rewarding him each time with the bright notes of her laughter. And she shooed away the little snowflakes on his lapels every five minutes. And that was love. Six years ago, when they were married, he was a slender saxophone player, with graceful curls and promise adorning his bright head. Even a year ago she could still make out her former Erik behind the balding, pasty banquet hall musician. That Erik—a princely sapling, soft and polite, in a paisley shirt and blue jeans and fiery curls cascading to his shoulders. They met in Sochi, signed the papers in Kiev, but the wedding feast had to wait until New York, until a tiny restaurant just down the street from their apartment in Astoria.

Strolling together they sent forth a kind of radiance. Preschoolers offered them their gapped smiles. Cats attended them everywhere. At the pizza shop on 32nd and Broadway they always got more change than they deserved. Not that it doesn't happen to everyone once or twice, but nearly every time—the reader will agree—is highly unusual. Let's say they order two slices of Neapolitan with olives and mushrooms. One dollar seventy-five times two comes to three dollars fifty. Plus a giant diet Coke—they always got one to share—that's a dollar twenty-five. He extended a ten-dollar bill to the perennially unshaven, white-aproned Stan. And Stan, after giving the cash register a series of quick punches, counted out their change: a five bill, two singles and a quarter (total: seven twenty-five). But it should have been five twenty-five. This happened nearly every time. At the end of the exchange Stan always winked—first to her, then also to him—and croaked, "Buon appetito!"

All of a sudden the restaurant burned to the ground—the one where he played on Thursdays, Fridays and Saturdays. But someone said it wasn't so sudden. The owners, so they said, went through some sort of calculation and it was clear that the insurance money would come out three times as much as their annual take. Simple math. One Saturday he came home—not at three, as usual, but at eleven thirty—black from soot, clutching his charred sax to his chest. She heard the door creak, tossed aside *Anna Karenina*, jumped from the bed and ran into the hallway.

"What happened?" she asked. "Where is the case?"

"Burned," he whispered, sank into a chair by the coat rack and wept. She rushed to him, kissed his moist cheeks, then climbed into his lap and started to undo his green bowtie. She had given it to him on his thirtieth birthday.

For two and a half months he looked for another gig. Finally her friend Jill set him up with the ad agency where she worked. At first he thought little about the job, then he grew to hate it. On Saturdays, when wife and daughter went to the park—or weeknights, while she fetched the girl from practice—he took the saxophone down from the closet and went to the window to play. He had scrubbed off most of the soot with a special solution. As he played his thoughts traveled high above the wet tenement roofs, beyond the dark lindens, toward a park, where snowbanks lay frozen beneath scraps of clouds. He played and his fingers just barely kept with the movement of his thoughts, and his thoughts were not of things as they were, but of things as they had been or might have been, if it had all worked out in another way, since he wouldn't have had to leave, he could have stayed and had his speech therapy degree by now—her father promised to help with a job once he was done; could have won a camera through the lottery and gone to heaven; *preferans* with wife's friends in the summer—she could be genuinely concerned: don't sit in the sun, you'll get burned; many things would be transformed into habit—like "dinner is ready"; she—the other one—wouldn't come to him in the night so often, and then she could also laugh, not at him, but down there by the rocks; she could have loved him, and tears would come all on their own, and the lump in the throat also; Jews could learn not to torture their R's and Russians not to stutter after the third and Uzbeks not to eat rice with their hands so much. How did it go now? Kefir in the morning, first you have to shake it for a long, long time—shake well—and then pop the green foil lid with your thumb—hop. Holland cheese with tea in the evening—hop two. But that's mostly about eating. Always making generalizations—that isn't useful. Yes, there were many good things, dog poop aplenty, too. The evenings in May were cool and the wind came some place from the sea; the 1st of May tableau was really just many lightbulbs put together, and read backwards it would be Ram 1. We were all going crazy over that album, and so we smiled at one another across the falling dusk: we liked to think that the town elders shared our tastes, if only backwards, never really aware of it, but still they were in it too. Everything could have turned out differently. But it didn't, meaning, perhaps, that it couldn't have. All things being equal—that's just the way it is in math, but in life she could have broken her heel a month later, and then he wouldn't carry her in his arms up the stairs that Sunday and her eyes wouldn't shine the way they did on that night in June. And her name could have been something other than Inga, but rather Agnia, or something. But who can say—the best of times: is it already past, or is it sill ahead? Is it something that could have been, or is it something that is—here and now, at this window, saxophone in hand? Who can say? Not I.

And now a hand flies up all the way in the back of the class-room—the hand of a new boy in a comic waistcoat. And every-one turns to see. And the teacher tells him: yes, go ahead, Erik. And Erik, with a nervous stutter—or is it an ancient impedi-ment?—gets up and says in a hollow sort of voice, "I feel like the best is still the head of us!" and he turns absolutely bright red. And suddenly everyone is laughing. The teacher is laughing. And the new boy is laughing with them. And the laughter all around him grows bigger and bigger. And the laughter is at once inside of him and outside, and out the window, over by the lindens in the park, and even farther down. And he sees two figures—one big and the other just tiny—crossing the street in the falling dusk, and the two of them are looking at him, and then at each other, and the big figure hunches its shoulders and shakes its head, while the little figure is waving at him and smiling, and he waves back, nodding, still playing.

*translated by Sergey Levchin*

# The Foreskin

I haven't touched a pen in some time now; more than that—I've had the persistent feeling that somebody had written about it before. Where? When? I couldn't say. Did I write it? If it was me then it must have been some time after '83. That's when I started writing—May of 1983—exactly sixteen years ago. Of course, that isn't exactly true. I was writing even before that, but it was all poetry. Poetry isn't serious; moreover, in my case it had a strictly therapeutic function. I was having an especially painful recovery after a break from a certain party, aged twenty-four, with a tiny scar just under her lip. I poured out my shredded feelings in dismal verse, some of which I transcribe below, by way of adverse example:

> An average-looking man swings an axe, left-right.
> There is a vacuum howls in his heart.
> He screams, "You whore!"
> Whereas his bloodied wife collapses by and by.

At this point my sparse audience typically broke in to ask, "How is that—collapses by and by? Explain!" I explained patiently that the woman was hacked into several pieces, which fell to the floor at different rates.

> This dreadful scene before me—did I invent it?
> Did Schopenhauer? That's inessential.
> The man goes muttering something to himself;
> his thoughts, like Proust, flow inward and then outward.

What Proust has to do with it, or Schopenhauer, for that matter—I couldn't tell you. Like I said, it wasn't serious. I concluded the piece with my own tortured variation on the perennially passé "Exegi monumentum":

> Proust-shmoust, Cherchez la femme perdue, et al.
> Whatever for? What shall escape the pyre?
> Yet I may here and there go on living
> in some such places and discrete locales.

Faced with the foregoing the reader will agree, I think, that I did not start writing in earnest until 1983, and that in all likelihood any previous attempts to set down the story were lost, when in 1985 I was preparing to take up residence (permanent, I thought) in a different state, where, upon arrival, I found myself short two boxes: one of them contained various kinds of dishware, bought on sale from Macy's (San Francisco, Union Sq.), the other—underwear and notebooks. Dishware can be replaced, of course (was replaced by Conran's on 3rd Ave), but underwear and notebooks are a different story.

And even if the manuscript of the tale relating an episode in the life of my friend P.L. was not among the papers lost in the move, having gone through my archives a good number of times, I have no other choice but to conclude that it is not in my possession.

I would finish this already drawn out preface with one last comment: if at some point in the past I did in fact set down these events—which seem to me remarkable even today—then it is also likely that the manuscript was destroyed (if not lost in the move) by my own hand.

I could not say precisely why I did it, but I would like to propose a few possible motives. For one thing, I was somewhat more critical of my own stuff in the early days. I had dubbed my method "writing against the grain." The reader may make of it what he likes: self-discipline, self-confidence (lack of), a hyperactive left hemisphere, etc., etc. These days I am far more at peace with myself—everyone is granted a certain measure of talent, and I know where I stand in that regard. My ambitions are reasonable, my scruples are moderate—I'm not going to kill myself over every word, I'll take it as it comes. Even if on occasion I may slip over the boundaries of good taste and propriety, I never cross it out, I leave the dirty bits out in the open because, as a writer, I write what I please, even the dirty bits. And so it is with the good ladies and gentlemen readers of these lines: each has his dirty bits, and I could even point them out, if necessary. Yes, we all have them—can't live without them. Therefore, don't let yourself skim over those bits: the life in them is real, the pain is real—when the anesthetic wears off.

And the last thing: if I have never yet sat down to write this tale—never lost it, never destroyed it with my own hands—if I am writing it all down for the first time (though I doubt it) then there is yet another explanation: perhaps it is because I have carried the story within me far too long that I have come to think of it as a thing in the world, a thing that I have already thrust out into the world once before.

The thing itself, however—the triangle—because the story begins and ends with this geometrical figure—may be readily found in a variety of places, e.g. in every household Mérimée: a certain marquis, whose name escapes me, is in love with his wife, who—in turn—has developed a questionable attachment to an officer atop a purebred colt. A naïve story, to be sure, but the Frenchman did paint in bold strokes, the characters are done in high relief—you can't take that away from monsieur Mérimée.

In film the theme was treated reasonably well by Hitchcock. In one of his pictures—the name escapes me—Ingrid Bergman seduces, then marries a certain spineless Nazi, while Cary Grant, playing an American spy, takes it upon himself to oversee the operation. Predictably, Grant soon finds himself falling helplessly for Bergman's charms and the situation turns outright explosive when it is discovered that the wine bottles in the good Nazi's cellar are filled with uranium.

Consequently, my readers may rest assured that I didn't one day invent the classic triangle. P.L., on the other hand—the hero of my tale—had first discovered its curious geometry at an early age, and later was deposited squarely at its apex.

For, as the story goes, before New York P. L. was living in Odessa (Karl Liebknecht St.) and spending a good deal of his time with a pretty girl from a decent family. Their parents were friendly. More than friendly, it seems, since the girl's father had a thing for P.L.'s mother, and the thing was returned. One day they had breakfast together and then got down under the table. This was about noon. Suddenly there was the sound of footsteps in the hallway. The mother sprang to her feet and started fixing her hair, whereas the girl's father proceeded into the bathroom to freshen up. P.L.'s father entered the room. Work ended early that day on account of death in the management. He gave his wife a sidelong glance and drew the air in stiffly several times. Then he too proceeded into the bathroom. Within a few moments hell was ready to break loose. The neighbors had to call the cops in on this Mérimée...

Need I say that in the aftermath of this episode P.L.'s mother divorced his father, the girl's father divorced his wife, and P.L. saw no more of the girl? Probably not.

A year later he found himself in New York. Ah, States United, home of the potato! The endlessly variegated display of canned products is too much for words. And the automobiles! Ford LTD, Buick LeSabre, Ford Mustang... No, you couldn't count them all, shouldn't try even.

P.L. and I met at Queens College, where both of us sat in on lectures in Art History in the spring semester. It turned out that we shared a number of vital statistics (age, birthplace, etc.) and felt equally disoriented, if not outright lost, in the new world, away from the friends and places we once knew. We came together quickly and clung to each other like two drowning men, each thinking the other to be the better swimmer. We were inseparable: cramming for tests, feeding youthful curiosity at movie houses in Times Sq., eating lunch between lectures, etc.

One day as we sat in the cafeteria, ham-and-cheeses in hand, P.L. decided to pour out his heart to me.

"You'll probably say I jumped the gun — so began his tale — You're more cautious than me when it comes to such things. You'd have looked twice before jumping. I didn't. You know, I can never tell with them if I should still be going with: 'Every Angel is terrible. . .' or moving on to 'How do you get that thing off?' But that time I just up and came out with it. No, not 'What are you doing later on?' — that would have been more or less within the norm. . .

"She was a doctor in torn heavy knit socks. This detail I picked up some time later. Long legs, blue eyes, physical surgery. I lay before her like an open book — she was just finishing up then. True, I was under local, but my head was ringing like it was all-out general. Two weeks later, when I had already made it through 'Every Angel is terrible. . .', she claimed that I was winking at her from the operating table. It's a nervous tick I have — standard complications. Of course, she did look cute in her facemask, and I in my oxygen. I was pretty happy with the cut, though it made peeing difficult at first. Circumcision. So much packed into a single word. She looked like Onassis. No, not Jackie, his mom. Not a great beauty, but super fine features. Even after the anesthetic wore off I didn't take it back. What did I tell her? I'm getting there. Backstory first.

"As you well know I do my bit as a cabby. My nails may not be in best shape, I'll give you that, but I scrub my pony clean after every shift. My partner is pretty clean too. Occasionally you run into Indians of that persuasion. I call him Joe—that's not his real name, though; his real name I can't pronounce. I tried: Rakhtanakhbhapal, Bakhtarakhnaphal, I don't know, Singh something. Basically, I can't do it, that's really all. He doesn't mind. I don't mind it either, since he's chosen to forgo my own given name and also calls me Joe. I understand that it makes things easier for him. Joe and I share a cab—I have the night shift. The owner of the car is an Israeli guy, Yehuda Shloma something Benvenir, not really Benvenir. Basically, I don't remember. We decided to call him Joe also—not to his face, though—he's jumpy. Joe and I aren't looking for trouble.

"Now, how did I ever get the idea to shed my foreskin? This was largely Joe's doing; not Indian Joe, Israel Joe, and not so much him as a certain lady friend from Kharkov. They came over about two years ago. Israel Joe's been on my case from day one: are you Jewish? you wanna go to shul with me? you wanna go to Israel? you believe in God? Meanwhile, last summer I was seeing a girl from Kharkov that was one of them. One Saturday we went to a birthday party; with the festivities going strong she was just about to slide my member into her mouth, when something happened. She said, 'Hmm, Pavel, you seem to be uncircumcised.' 'Right you are,' said I and made an inviting gesture with my thing. In response she pulled up her pants and said earnestly, 'Pasha, you're a Jew. Jews and foreskins don't mix.' 'Why you, rotten cunt!' I said, overcome with feeling, 'You're going to deny me my pleasure over this shit, you such-and-such!' 'Shut your fuck trap, Pasha,' she said. 'Get circumcised, or you can start blowing it yourself. . .'

"At this point a number of guests popped their heads into the room, and I thought it wise to cut the conversation short.

"The next day I went up to Israel Joe and asked him where I could get myself circumcised quickly. 'Mazel tov!' exclaimed Joe and went in for a hug. I was informed that circumcisions were free at select locations. I called the number Joe had given me and made an appointment (Thursday, I think). Indian Joe volunteered to drive me over. I told him I'll cover waiting time, but he waved me off and promised to return for me after the operation. 'Have no 100 rubles, but have 100 friends!' I told him in Russian and followed with a loose translation, to which he nodded emphatically. Turns out they have a similar saying in his country.

"Thursday morning we drove to Bensonhurst, left our buggy in the hospital lot, disconnected the meter and walked toward the grey four-story building.

'What seems to be the trouble?' asked the lady.

'Foreskin,' said I and started filling in the registration form.

"There were about six of us in the reception room: a frightened boy about eight years old and his parents, who were having a protracted and loud argument; an old man in a bow tie and snow-white tennis shoes worn over bare feet; a grungy looking lardy young man with a volume of early Pynchon in his lap, plus a few others. Indian Joe stayed with me a few minutes for politeness' sake, then wished me luck, and advised me to watch that they don't cut off any more than necessary.

"'Won't be too easy,' said I vaguely. I was starting to get a bit worried about the operation. Still, the next hour or so spent in the waiting room went by quickly on account of the old man in tennis shoes. Turned out he had spent forty-five years as a street magician, and he offered to raise our spirits with a few signature tricks. He started off with silk scarves, which disappeared and reappeared unexpectedly, sometimes separately, sometimes tied together; for the finale he asked the quarrelsome pair to tie three scarves into a ball, stuffed it into his mouth, then motioned for the little boy to undo his (the old man's) trousers; when the boy finally agreed, the old man reached into his gaping fly and produced a smallish grey dove. The frightened bird made a few circles around the waiting room, dropped a few bullets on early Pynchon, and finally settled on the magician's shoulder. By then there was nothing in his mouth. Everyone applauded the performance, the old man took a bow, zipped up his pants and sat down next to me, launching into a leisurely discourse on the conservation of matter. Turned out that he did not accept this phenomenon. At first I tried to argue politely, then I got annoyed and even tried to drag in my stepfather, who had taught high school physics at some point; he and my mom got married shortly before we left.

"'And what does your stepfather do these days?' asked the old man.

"'He has his own business,' I said.

"'What is that, may I ask?'

"'You may,' I said. 'He sells hotdogs on 41st and Lexington.'

"'No further questions,' smiled the old man, pleased at something. I was about to ask him what he meant by that smile, and what it had to do with the conservation of matter, but just then the door opened and somebody called out my name.

"I won't go into the details of the procedure; the effect of this story doesn't depend on your ability to visualize my bloodied member or experience the kind of masochistic curiosity with which I followed the surgeon's precise movements. I'll skip ahead to the words that flew from my parched lips in the moments just before the incision, and which had such an effect on the young doctor. 'Pardon me,' I said. 'You will probably think my request a bit strange, but I would like to have something as a memento of today's events, provided everything goes smoothly. Would you please let me keep my foreskin?' Lisa (that was the doctor's name) nearly dropped her scalpel, and her blue eyes got very big. 'Yes,' I continued, 'you heard me correctly. I want to keep something in memory of our meeting today.' She didn't say anything. I couldn't even tell if she smiled under her facemask.

"Then the operation was over. Lisa's assistant gave me a half glass of red wine and patted me on the shoulder, mumbling something in Yiddish.

"For about two hours I lay in recovery, listening to the cries of the small boy—the one who undid the magician's pants, and who had gone in before me. When the anesthetic wore off I felt the kind of pain I never felt before. I cursed the day I was born, the day I came to this country, and the eighth day on which I was not circumcised like the majority of god-fearing Jews. I also cursed the girl from Kharkov and her goddam convictions.

"Half an hour later Indian Joe stuck his head in from behind the curtain. He helped me get up from the bed and get dressed, then led me slowly toward the exit, coaching me, as we went: 'That's good, Joe, keep it up, Joe, just a bit more, easy does it. . .' A handsome black nurse greeted me in the reception room. She handed me a small plastic jar, and I saw my own foreskin floating there in a hazy solution. It seemed to me like some fantastic sea creature. I thanked the nurse, and we went out.

"I was glad to find the taxi waiting just outside the glass doors. Israel Joe smiled at me from behind the wheel and got out to help. He and Indian Joe were able to maneuver me into the back seat.

"Riding back to Queens I couldn't take my eyes off the little plastic jar. Now I imagined my foreskin to be the brain of a tiny creature sent here by a civilization many light years away, and it was about to communicate a very important piece of information. I remember pressing the jar to my ear in order to hear the message better, but the foreskin kept silent.

"We were already turning onto Kissena Blvd., when I happened to glance at the lid. There was a message, written in a hurried scrawl: 'Do they let morons get circumcised? Call me when you feel better.' Then followed a number and the name: Dr. Lisa Lewis.

"The rest is history. Four days later the bandages came off, and two days after that I went back to work. On Saturday I finally got up the nerve and dialed her number. She was glad to hear I was doing fine, she said, and we agreed to have dinner at a Japanese place on 46th St.

"She turned out to be a charming, intelligent girl, crazy about poetry, especially 'Every Angel, etc.' Apparently she thought my operating table antics so retarded she was shaking with laughter for about five minutes—scalpel in hand. You can imagine the kind of danger I was in. . . After that we started seeing each other. I wasn't going to call my Kharkov flame, but one day she called up all on her own and demanded to know why I'd fallen off the face of the earth. I tried to explain to her the specific time constraints associated with work and school, etc., which had very little effect on her. She insisted she had to see me—at my place.

"Once in she got down to business, 'You had it done?' I pretended not to know what she was talking about. For some reason she didn't believe me and asked for material evidence. Reluctantly I complied. Seeing the naked lie she became furious, slammed her fist on my desk and demanded to know the name of her rival. I assured her that she had no rival, that since the operation I've been avoiding social contact, especially with women, especially the kind that barge in and start banging on furniture; and moreover I had to work in the evening and required rest. 'I see,' she said, getting up from her chair. She started pacing up and down the room, like she was looking for something. Suddenly she saw a little plastic jar that I had left on top of the piano, next to a vase of bohemian crystal. She snatched the jar and saw the note on the lid, which sent her into convulsions. She was howling with laughter. I asked her to leave the jar where it was and to cut the hysterics. In response she stuck out her tongue, made an untranslatable hand gesture (like the tongue hadn't been sufficiently expressive), and ran out, slamming the door.

"Then what happened? About a week later Lisa comes over and tells me she's being crank-called: apparently a man had been calling her for the past three days, speaking bad English, and saying he is about to file a complaint against her for violating ethical standards, professional conduct norms, etc. I advised Lisa to ignore this nonsense, and mentioned that I suspected I knew the responsible party.

"'How am I supposed to ignore it,' asked Lisa, 'when I get calls at one in the morning? What if he actually starts calling my work? You have to put an end to it!'—she was close to shouting. Knowing Lisa to be a generally restrained and balanced person I surmised that this time she was fairly pissed off.

"The next day I made my way to the Kharkovite's apartment in the Bronx and demanded that she stop harassing decent people in the middle of the night by way of illiterate accomplices, return my foreskin and cut out the crap generally. In response she started by cursing at me, but quickly resolved into sobbing. I made an effort to console her, patting her on the shoulder, to which she sobbed even louder.

"'Look at me, for Christ's sake,' I said. 'Is this ugly mug really worth extreme emotional suffering?' Unexpectedly, the last argument struck home. She pointed at me her teary eyes, gave a final sob and emptied her nose into a tissue. 'You're right, you know. Who needs you? Take your snippet—it's in the fridge—and fuck off. You and your American whore, both of you...'"

Here P. L. interrupted his tale, because we were already considerably late for 20th c. art. We made to look embarrassed coming into the lecture hall, but the professor didn't even turn to us—his thoughts were deep in Duchamp's great Fountain that had once caused such an uproar among the good citizens of Paris.

Is there anything else? P.L. married Lisa and the two moved out to Connecticut, to take over an old house that had belonged to her grandfather. P.L. got his Ph.D. and then a professorship at Columbia, where his latest offering is titled "Negation of art autonomy and the principles of trans-postmodernism." One late night a few years ago Indian Joe was shot in the stomach while trying to protect his cab—he had just bought it out from Israel Joe. The Israeli bought a small deli in Soho and seems to be doing well. The Kharkov flame studied computer science and now runs IT for a New York bank. I've been putting off a visit to Connecticut for the last three or so years, despite a standing invitation from Lisa and P.L. I'm waiting for the wounds to heal—the ones that came with the break from a certain party, aged twenty-four, with a tiny scar just under the lip. Maybe then I could finally bear to look upon the happily married, perhaps even consider joining their ranks at some distant point. Whether it's a triangle or a parallelogram—I don't care; as long as there's a vacant corner I can claim for myself. I'm tired of this lonely posture—this bare perpendicular, stuck in the middle of nowhere. Perpendicular to what? To a plane? A point? Is there a point, I'm asking you?

*translated by Sergey Levchin*

# 2 Sisters

Take a minute to look around and you will see right away that life is far from senseless. On the contrary, life is full of meaning. If I may be permitted a minor witticism, it is a senseless man that calls life senseless. The story that was told to me by the late Tim O.—chess master, ladies' man, Cuban jazz aficionado, all-around solid guy—will serve nicely to illustrate the point.

Two sisters lived in New York: East Side—West Side. This was back in the late eighties. Real beauties: lovely curves, rosy cheeks, natural blondes, quick eyes, sharp tongues—everything. How they moved! they shimmied, and discoed, and jitterbugged, and even did the slam dance at the Tunnel, way past late. They could do a headstand and boy, were they sassy! One of them went crazy for *raki* (lobsters in English, said her sister), the other couldn't go a day without *kolbasa* (salami in English, said her sister). Drove the male contingent positively wild—the contingent tucked its gut, flared its nostrils, twitched uncontrollably, barked at intersections, offered its services at the gym (handle that dumbbell? reach that rack?) et cetera. The girls liked the attention, blushed a little for politeness' sake, but the act went no further. They'd had a proper upbringing: the basic need for companionship and sexual gratification did not translate for them into random encounters with questionable types, who, as a rule, kept an old goat up each armpit at all times. And though one of the sisters worked for an escort service (that's just how it played out for her) and the other was a starving bohemian—neither was a stranger to real emotional need, and each in her own way despised the brute sex.

That's just what they were talking about over dinner one April evening.

"I tell you, I can't stand them. They reek of sewage—slob, neat-freak, they all have the stench on them. I'm not exaggerating. There he is: freshly shaven, hair slicked back, running off to his place of business, stroking his paycheck (mentally)—starched, pressed, a walking Brooks Brothers catalog—and I'm telling you, I can smell him from over here: he stinks like the outhouse, smoker, non-, whatever. I'm not even talking about clients now. You'd better hold on to your saints when these boys start pulling off their breeches. I don't know about you, but I've been thinking about it, and there's no way I'm falling for this scam. I'll work as long as I can, and when that's done I'll buy a stake in the service. And if I ever want a baby—there's plenty of ways around that too. Somebody feels like getting in bed with bowel movement every night for the rest of their lives—that's their business. But it's a sick business, if you're asking me. Eat, child. What's the matter?"

"Oh, nothing," began the bohemian sister cheerlessly, "I'm not so crazy about them either, you know. We had a new model in the studio recently—Tim. Crazy tattoos, piercings all over the place, built out—you know—*bicepsi-tricepsi*, everything in the right place, a specimen. Anyway, wants to get coffee. I'm thinking: maybe never. He insists—I demur. So he gets the bright idea: starts twitching with this thing or that thing while he's posing. Basically, he's screwing me up—I can't concentrate. The whole studio is only four people: Dan, two old bags and yours truly. They're all conceptualists, anyway, and one of the old bags is basically blind. They don't give a damn whether he's twitching or doing cartwheels up there. I'm the only one that has to suffer—because I have this cursed realist strain. I'm the only one that needs him to stand still, for christ's sake, because I still have some respect for the human anatomy. I believe the body is a viable object of representation. In the end I thought: fine, coffee is coffee, it's not carnal knowledge. So we ended up getting coffee in the West Village."

"Where? Sha-Sha?"

"No, there's another place that just opened up, basically next door. Anyway, we get our cappuccino, macchiato, rum-baba, tra-la-la, where you're from, California, studied acting, but nothing so far. I tell him: could you get into commercials, or is that also dry? You know what he says? I want you to hurt me—I'll tell you where exactly, and what boots and stockings you'll be wearing, my lizard-child, and then we'll make like two preschoolers, ok? Lizard-child? Preschoolers? I say, I'm sorry—I have no idea what you're talking about. So he starts explaining to me exactly what his thing is, and when he must have it (immediately), he's just up here on 8th Street. I'm ready to vomit. Charming young fellow."

"What's his thing, anyway?" The other one was a professional and she'd run into all kinds of unusual requests. Sometimes she was even moved to grant them, though it was always extra.

"I can't—not at the table. Trust me, it's vile enough. I ran out, sprinting down Hudson, no umbrella—it's raining like hell—I had an umbrella but it was broken, and I just couldn't get it to open, because it's just pouring. He starts after me—he's pretty athletic, obviously—caught me at Bank St., I'm screaming like mad—basically, he's trying to shove his tongue in my mouth—I whack him with the umbrella. Next thing, he pulls this giant you know what I mean out of his backpack, there's water everywhere, drags me into a doorway, the specials are pretty decent, they brought out the *raki*, leave it on, like that, and the service is not like Chanterelle, let me tell you, but I'm not proud, just asked if they could bag it, for emotional stability, and that's without any sort of discursive probing! so, we ended up not calling the cops, with bare hands, split the bill, I took down his info, a small dent in the rear fender, could have been worse, with the belts on. Next time keep your eyes open, Mr. Blind Faith!"

"*Lobsters* in English," said her sister. What a dumb habit, always lecturing people, and way off, most of the time. She had clients that won't be lying down for it.

"*Kolbasa*. Can't stand them. Our parents (yes, their parents!) wouldn't let us, maintained precise genetic balance, kept under wraps, treated like equals, what grass? beer on very special occasions. Couple of tabs on July 4th. So much for wild years. One Christmas brought home a boy, wrote poetry with a limp. An average sort of boy. Acne, sweaters, early Jarmusch, Lacan, Mike Kelley. A bit of a limp, though."

"*Salami*! Not *raki*."

"What's on, anyway?"

"Bowel movement, Seinfeld, etc."

"And yet I believe that man as object of representation shall continue for some time."

"Knowledge, sweetheart, not representation."

"All the same."

"Not all. And you have to start with yourself."

"I wouldn't be starting with you, or your Delphic mama!"

"And what about yours? Huh? What about yours?"

And the sisters were suddenly shaking with laughter. And they went round and round the table like a twister—because the table was small, just for two—until they fell to the floor and just stayed there for the night (though they did try breaking to Sting first). There they were—two beauties, long lashes, delicate ear lines, half-parted carmine lips, dazzling teeth, little barbs in their tongues, magnificent hips—still, with somewhat troubled personal lives.

But was it the East Side or the West Side, I don't know. Tim O. never got around to that part. Anyway, he wasn't especially open about these things. He died while filming a miniseries on the fishermen of Long Island. It may have been a small part, but he took it seriously. I especially remember one scene: a close-up of his face, there is a kind of look in his eyes—part terror, part ecstasy. The camera pulls back: his hand is on his chest, he is sinking down onto a rock, deep in his own thoughts. . . Very realistic.

*translated by Sergey Levchin*

# Snoopy Goes to Kasimov

I used to torture myself over the question, I was baffled by it: to what could I attribute the incontrovertible fact of my total lack of literary talent? A fluke of nature? Blind chance? Genetic aberration? And this in a family tree, mind you, that's produced five writers minimum, two of which, in the opinion of their contemporaries, made a sizable contribution to the treasure house of Russian belles-lettres. My grandfather, who during his lifetime was honored with two major awards and several prizes for his literary achievements, wrote a dozen or so novels and screenplays, and in his capacity as an outstanding engineer of the human soul was buried with full honors at Novodevichy cemetery. My samizdat father couldn't get published for a long time; they came to their senses in the early sixties and started publishing him, then they stopped again, but nowadays, thanks to the enlightened eighties, it suddenly turns out that he was a fairly mediocre writer, and now his labor-camp prose, a cut below Shalamov's and almost as boring as Solzhenitsyn's, is safely gathering dust in central and peripheral Dom Knigi bookstores alike. And really, how can he hold a candle to Jackie Collins and Sidney Sheldon? For entertainment value and insider Hollywood knowledge, I mean.

But this story isn't about my father and grandfather. And not even about my grandfather's cousin, the people's poet Ignat Timofeich, who wrote all those marvelous songs during the war, and then marched into Berlin where not long after the Yalta Conference he opened a little cafe on Kurfurstendamm called Chez Ignaz, still going strong. This story is about me. About who I was before the concert and who I became after it.

I grew up as a carefree child of Litfond, my relatives paved the way ahead, and thanks to my grandfather's connections I had a brilliant career in store; at the beginning of perestroika I found myself in a small college town on the east coast of America, where I was studying economics along with the other fortunate few who had landed a spot on a university exchange program. Perhaps I didn't yet have a precise macro-goal, but I did have a number of micro-objectives in its stead. For example, not flunking finals, going to the right place on break, doing the right things around Americans to feel like their kind of guy, or at least to let them know that I was their kind of guy but still my own man etc. The majority of the micro-objectives were eminently doable: my classes weren't difficult; time flew by almost imperceptibly; the fruits of Americanization were there for all to see: pizza, beer, weed, and Saturday morning cartoons were now an integral part of my life in the West. Plus if you add in a rather favorable success rate among my openminded female classmates, who found "that Russian guy's" attentions rather engaging, then it will be quite clear, I hope, that I wasn't especially homesick for our three-room digs on Zemlyanoi Val in Moscow. And besides, in practically every letter from my parents they were sounding the alarm about THE THINGS that were going on at home, you'd have to be God knows what kind of idiot to come back RIGHT NOW. Just sit tight there at your college, they wrote, and not a peep out of you. Here I should note that I myself had come to the same conclusion, and had already sent out my applications to a number of prestigious schools in the hope that my grade-point average, letters of recommendation, and personal charm upon being interviewed would produce the desired impression on at least one of the admissions committees in one of the graduate schools in economics or business administration or whatever—and they would have to accept me. Which would mean two or three more years of clear sailing in the US. Who would have thought that fate would throw me head first into an entirely different scenario?

My latest girlfriend invited me to a concert on Saturday, the Grateful Kennedys or something like that. Before the concert, as per usual, we stop in at Häagen-Dazs for some frozen yogurt, I try to pay, she of course refuses (the babes here are awfully independent, not like at home), we get into her old Plymouth, and we have a nice chat along the way: "Do you have yogurt in Russia?" "Yes, we do," I answer, and at this point she offers me a little scrap of paper the size of a baby's fingernail, no bigger. On the scrap is a picture of Snoopy in dark glasses. "What's this?" I ask. "Acid," she replies. "What kind of acid?" "Acid acid, LSD, are you from outer space or what?" she says, sticks out her tongue, and puts an identical scrap of paper onto it. "And what happens?" I ask. "It'll be a lot of fun," she promises, swallows the paper, and adds mysteriously, "on the molecular level." "OK," I think, "this'll be interesting."

We pull into the stadium where the Talking Kennedys are supposed to be playing, I swallow the Snoopy paper and... nothing happens really, except maybe I feel a little warmer. We go into the auditorium, find our seats, granted, they're a long way from the stage, but Naomi brought binoculars, the crowd is whistling, the musicians are coming onstage one by one, and I also notice that one of them is wearing an outfit the color of meat with veins running through it, and he's fidgeting a lot, but the crowd is ecstatic, and the musicians are starting to twitch and flip around, but diagonally instead of upside down, and that's when I had the urge. "Where are you going?" I hear Naomi's voice somewhere above me, but instead of answering I lay one finger on her lips and walk forward into the darkness, tripping over somebody's feet, trying to steer by the Exit sign, and then the Toilets, and then the Men, and I think, "God, everything's all so messed up and confused, all these signs! And

each one of them means something! There's something or someone behind each one! This one for example, what's it supposed
to mean? That some men are waiting for me behind that door,
is that it? And what the hell do I need men for? I've gotta piss."
In short, I'm standing there in front of the door that says Men,
I stand there for an hour or so and don't know what to do to save
my life. Finally, I make up my mind to look in on them (although
I have to admit I was really tempted by the Women) and along
with me some thirty people squeeze in, and most of them are
these mirror guys, especially down there, like in a kaleidoscope,
but without so many facets, and here I am looking down the uri-
nal and not believing my eyes. It's all true, macro divided by mi-
cro equals mucro with almost no remainder, I'd known it deep
down all along, sixth sense, but just now did the exact calculation, and I—well, *I'm* Snoopy, they just pulled a switch, doesn't
take them long, you don't have to be a genetic engineer from
Stanford to know that. That is, it was me stuck on the piece of
paper in dark glasses and scarf, and me swallowing myself, and
these doors of course aren't really doors but just blinds and where
it says Exit you enter and where it says Entrance you exit, thank
God I figured that out! And the tile! The tile's cold! and the Dead
Kennedys are pounding out something really dark, really hos-
tile, really anti-establishment, but finding Naomi doesn't seem
very realistic, at least that's how it looks to me—she has the tickets—and I don't feel quite right here without her. Good thing I've
got some money in my pocket, a little wet and mucky but still
money, and a couple of credit cards, also damp, and now everything around me turns into dots, dot-to-dot just like Seurat, I'm
wagging my tail I'm so happy all of a sudden. And who cares how
I got to the airport?

On the plane I kept trying to work it out—which am I, a drawing or a print? If I'm a drawing, then how do I reproduce? Only
by means of a pencil, right? But better not think about that right

now. So—and this is essential—this means now I can put all my nose, my energy and talent (which is quite extraordinary even for a dog, you must agree) into the war on drug-arms-and-flesh trafficking. But where's the traffic? It's here, in my micro-power, my molecular motherland, understand? I even started salivating at the thought, and the guy sitting next to me moved to an empty seat by the Exit sign. My life suddenly seemed to have more color, more outline. A crystallization of the macro-meaning of it all. So what if I'm utterly devoid of literary talent? So what? Now I can be a catcher in the rye! If that's not a job for a hound, what is?

And I started waiting for my signal from the pilot. But it was no go. Yeah, the FBI's not too brilliant sometimes. The CIA's no ace at this either. There's a lot they just can't seem to get right. Plus the bureaucracy really is bloated and out of control; taxpayers' dollars really are being squandered. Good thing it's private-sector me footing the bill here, cute little caricartoon that I am. And then it struck me like a bolt from the blue: it's not the pilot—it's MURZILKA!*

I land in Moscow, take a cab from Sheremetyevo (outrageous, these prices, totally out of hand!) to Ryazan station and a train from there to Kasimov. Why Kasimov? Because Kasimov = i + mosKva, that's why. I mean you don't have to be a structural linguist from Harvard.

So. I'm sitting by the pissoir on the town square in Kasimov, waiting for agent M to establish contact—no sign so far. M was nowhere to be seen. At this point I was assailed by certain misgivings. Why did I eat myself on that paper, when Naomi's such a sweet little bitch with such nice chestnut hair and such a nice cold pug nose. No doubt she's searching for me high and low, whimpering. It's all like a dream, but I can't wake up. I wait for Murzilka. I wait one day, I wait two days.

---

* Murzilka: a Russian comic strip character.

Meanwhile, it's already October and the mornings are cold, and I can see my breath, and the railings on the wooden bridge on Sverdlov Street are covered with a thin layer of frost, and the old geezers at the beer stand by the market pull their "Barley Ear" bottles out of their bags and wink at each other and joke "Drink Barley Ear and have no fear," and rub their chilled hands together. In short, winter's almost here. And then I think, wait just a minute here. This must mean something. It's a password. That's it! Any minute now Murzilka, a shadowy figure in scarf and beret, will appear in the distance, look at me with those coal-black eyes of his, sit down beside me on my bench and say, looking off into the distance, "Drink Barley Ear." And I'll come right back with the countersign. And he'll shake my paw, scratch me behind the ear and give me detailed instructions on what I'm supposed to do next. Because otherwise I'll freeze here on this bench for dead sure, I will. Yeah, I know I'm just a drawing (or a print) but either way, it's very cold out. And I was drawn (or printed) above zero, but now we're obviously way way below.

But there he is, there's Murzilka! Finally—it's about time! Lord, he's so tiny! Well I'm no Hound of the Baskervilles either, I guess. What's that he's squeaking? Ah right, the password. Come again? Can't hear a thing. How do you turn him up? "Drink Heineken?" What's Heineken got to do with it? The password's "Drink Barley Ear"; the countersign is "and have no fear." What did they do, switch passwords at the last minute and forget about me? Or adjust for possible Western influence? This is a fine mess! What am I supposed to answer? I mean he could get up and leave. And then my God, I'll croak here in Kasimov, I mean my money's running out and I have no idea where their safe houses are. "Drink Heineken," Murzilka repeats, and shoots me a side-long glance. I've got to come up with an answer! Some answer, any answer, just so long as it rhymes! But what's a Russian rhyme for Heineken? There isn't one? What a disaster! Uncle Ignat from

Berlin, that's who I need here, he'd find a rhyme in two shakes. *Ich habe kein eineken, zweineken, dreineken.* This is ridiculous. I'm starving. And now he's getting up. He's going away. He's turning the corner by the store. No! I can't just let him go like that! I can't. If I let him go, then what's left for me—going "shoppink" and to "parteez," watching TV and pretending to be an American?

"Hey, pal, wait, where you going? I came all the way from Stony Brook to get here. On the Long Island Expressway. See, friend, I didn't know they'd switched the password. I didn't. Nobody warned me about that. What am I supposed to do next, eh? I don't know how things work here anymore, been away a long time, forgotten a lot. . . I'm up for any assignment you give me. Any and all! Just tell me my mission!? What brought me here? Who brought me here? Say something, Murzilka! Please!"

And at this point he turns around, stares straight at me like those coal-black eyes of his are taking my picture, adjusts his beret and says in a cold-roughened high-pitched little voice:

"Lord, what a dumbshit! What am I supposed to do with you, my American friend? Forgetting the countersign! That takes some doing. No wonder they say that as a nation you're generally a little dense. Although your Russian's all right. You could pass for a local. OK, then. Come on boy, heel, headquarters is right around the corner."

And so Murzilka and I quick-march toward the wooden bridge on Sverdlov, and on the way he gives me detailed instructions about my first assignment, and I feel like Savushkin* in *The Dead Season* and I nod my head eagerly, show my teeth, wag my tail and hang on his every word.

*translated by Jane Miller*

---

\* Savushkin: a reluctant, amateur agent from the Russian 1960s detective movie *The Dead Season.*

# Among the Stones

One man, far from old yet, loved to converse with plants. Another one, contradicting the first, found stones to be the more interesting companions. And that is from whom he had alleged to have heard the following story.

A giggly girl by the name of Martha was missing an index finger. During the summer, she wanted a child, and in the winter pure love; pure love in what sense? That would be without physical contact, with the eyes only, with breath, and phone calls, yeah?

She was awakened by the breath of spring.

Yesterday, with a boy, she headed into the depths of the park, to an aquarium where the fish stirred the water with their fins. An old woman was sitting nearby, her nose stuck in the newspaper. A typical, as it were, city landscape: dust, blue skies, pale green foliage, the jittery fish. Walking to the aquarium, the boy had put his hand around Martha's waist. They sat down on the bench, the fish stirring the water with their fins. She shut her eyes, he kissed her on her arid lips, and she threw her head back. Interesting, how would their relationship progress? Could it be: petty slights, quarrels, jealousy, tears? I would hope not.

The giggly girl scratched her shoulder. She was a zoologist. It was Saturday. She was feeling unwell. Yesterday, she had got soaked to the bone. It was half past eight.

Martha found the roach of a joint in the ashtray and a lighter in the drawer, clicked the lighter, lit up, and took a puff. She loved getting high first thing in the morning. The giggly girl put on headphones and turned up Steely Dan. The room was spinning. The chairs huddled against the wall. The ceiling seemed like it was on another planet. The keloids on Martha's wrists shone white. She had no idea what to do next and took the headphones off. This took place in Frankfurt, in the mid-80s, in a two-story house not far from the university. Giggly Martha was studying ornithology. She had a thing for larks. Her father had been a neo-Nazi, her mother, the widow of a neo-Nazi.

Martha headed for the bathroom. From the bathroom mirror, a face gazed at her severely. And who might this be? Ornithologist Martha Sch., the girl with the missing index finger, smallish, palish-pink nipples, daughter of a deceased neo-Nazi. In the bed, in her room, the boy had come to. Martha peeked out of the bathroom. The blanket had slipped off the boy and it made the girl smile. She proceeded to jump into the shower and scrub herself a long time with a sponge. It was now nine. She loved weekends.

Martha's boyfriend was a pretty decent lover; his member was pretty sizeable and Martha liked it. She would call him "Mein Führer," and referred to her lovemaking as "Mein Kampf." The boyfriend was unemployed, with a shaven head and a tattoo on his left buttock. Martha was tolerably good at checkers, and her mother taught German in an elementary school, even though her life-long dream was to have a career as a philosopher.

This story would be incomplete, if I were remiss in telling you the following: Martha's boyfriend's name was Karl, he treated her well and respected her. In a short time, Martha helped him get a job as a laboratory assistant at the university. At first he washed the glassware and test tubes, but then he was entrusted with the work of assisting in experiments on birds and mammals. In 1986, Karl married Martha and, in another year, they had a beautiful boy. In honor of the grandfather, they named the boy Stefan.

This story was overheard by my old acquaintance Joseph Weintraub among the stones, and he retold it to me under the strictest confidence, because he knew well that only a very few people might believe that stones can speak, and he had no desire to become the laughing stock of the town in his advanced years. I have now broken the solemn word I had given to him and am prepared to bear full responsibility for it.

Dear Joseph, if you are reading these lines, please know that, having decided to publish this story, I myself, vicariously as it were, now share in your conviction that stones can speak. Nevertheless, I ask your forgiveness yet again for breaking my word of honor and hope that our friendship will not suffer thereby.

*translated by Alex Cigale*

# Oleg, Mila, and I, and Honolulu, and the Korean

A girl with a pneumatic bust and a temperamental gait, having clenched her fists and knuckled down, decided to get married. What else is there to say; it's a good thing. She was a second year student on the Intravenous track and coughed reflexively, having noticed Oleg and I. Oleg, then, was prickly, but I was considerably kinder and more easygoing. I was indistinguishable from him, except on the charm front, but, and I repeat myself here, the girl with a pneumatic bust and a temperamental gait, having clenched her fists and knuckled down, decided to get married. What can I say; it's a good thing. At that time, as you might recall, it was fashionable to marry nurses like there was no tomorrow. Made sense, too: a nurse is a nurse, in Honolulu also. Well, Oleg, as you well know, was fantasizing then about Honolulu night and day, the topography, the local cocktails, language, dances—he wanted to have as complete an image of Honolulu as possible in advance, so that when he finally gets to this Honolulu... oh, right, not Honolulu; I've got it all wrong, I said: "A nurse is a nurse, in Honolulu also," and then took off on that tangent for Honolulu like a spooked horse, even though Oleg didn't dream about Honolulu or anything of the sort, but about the state of Georgia. He would sing the song about it, even two songs, and memorized the names of the last three presidents of the Coca-Cola company, the world headquarters of which, as you well know, is in the city of Atlanta, state capital of Georgia, ibid and etcetera. To make a long story short, we're sitting on the boulevard, strumming all sorts of rubbish on our guitars when, all of a sudden, we see three cats, two of whom I recognized from the neighborhood, one of them had relatives abroad, and he dressed. . . may God himself give you the chance to dress as stylie. Though once I wrote these words down, I reigned myself in. Or rather, started coughing. Just like our very own Mila from the Intravenous track. Such are the low-hanging fruit of an overly narrow specialization. Veins—could it be any narrower? Injections—that's too easy, where do you want it, and if bandaging is needed? And making a compress? Mila also wore flared pants. An energetic girl she was, she has two children by Oleg, who died last year under somewhat stupid circumstances (at least I suspect that the car accident was pre-arranged)—the older girl is now completing college. And she did it all by herself, all the responsibilities on her own back. These days, everyone wants everything as fast as possible and without any special efforts; hard work's not fashionable these days. Give it to me, give it to me—everybody wants something. Only one of the three was dressed in clothes sent to him from abroad, the other two were impeding me, blocked me, disrespected me, so there's no surprise what happened next—some things become clearer with time, other things less distinct, and styles have changed, and cocktails also—the times have changed, the calendar of days, laws and regulations, life is faster. I expect nothing from no one (what? from whom?) except respect, and not even as much for myself as for the memory of the deceased. The final remaining debt, do you see what I'm talking about? Flares had become fashionable again some five years ago, but Mila had so transparently hinted to me: "So OK, so what if I buy these flared pants by Ferré for four hundred dollars. In another year, nobody's gonna be wearing them, and I'll be left holding them like a complete idiot. . ." And I'm looking at her, I'm looking at her, and I think, and I think: well, what do I think? If only it was me—when she got married that it was to me, would it have been me dead in a car crash? No, it's just not wise to think this way. And I'm also thinking: Mila. . . And I toss and turn and can't fall asleep. Mila's now dating some Korean, a manager at a Coca-Cola plant. She coughed for about ten minutes, reflexively, trying to get his attention, until he, finally, offered her a glass of water. Of water! Then, he took her under her arm and accompanied her to the doors of the elevator. One day soon, they will, not unlikely, go out to dinner, at the same restaurant Oleg once worked in.

Honolulu, cough cough. It wouldn't kill her to go in for some x-rays, by the way.

*translated by Alex Cigale*

# Visiting the Girlfriends

One time, Volodya was invited to drop in on two girls of liberal views. One of them worked as a buyer at a book store and the other had formerly studied with him at a technical college. He had on a number of occasions helped this other one to get warm, in winter, when it was particularly drafty, but always under Platonic circumstances. How did he learn of their liberal views? After all, it's not something that's scribbled across a woman's forehead. They wore free-wheeling footwear, without back straps; only women with liberal views wore shoes like that. Very frank and open footwear. Their big toes would stick out obscenely through their big toe compartments, reminiscent of fat shrimp that had been plied and overstimulated with beer. And these girls were only too glad to swivel them about enticingly.

What did they have that evening, at the book buyer Rita's and engineer Sasha's apartment? They had white wine, inexpensive, three bottles, fried Russian dumplings, pirozhki, with meat and with potatoes, still warm, and chocolate bonbons, with nuts. Rita was a red-haired girl, who in her free time performed Ukrainian folk songs on a reed pipe. Engineer Sasha, a brunette with small and very firm breasts, preferred trip-hop. She fussed about more than her friend and smiled attractively, wanting Volodya more than her friend did. She really wanted to give it a go with him, having heard he was a lion in bed, thundering, tearing his quarry to pieces, dripping with hot seed, for some time after orgasming, jerking in spasms. And that's precisely what happened. He spewed over the entire couch, the wild-maned one, while the girls had him saddled.

They had met by chance, in a tram car. Volodya was riding to his job at the shooting gallery, and all of a sudden, dear God, Vovka, how many years it's been? Rita, Sasha, where are you off to? Work. Me too. Yes, yes. Such a dull, grown-up life. Do you remember. . . yes, let's. . . yes, tonight at Sasha's. This proposal came from Rita, the more confident one at lovemaking.

And the sunlight scatters in the tram's rear window. It seemed that they were as though in a dream, alone in the car. Sasha was drinking milk straight out of the glass bottle, a white trace of it staining her upper lip. Somebody will say something funny. And she erupts in a coruscation of giggles. The sound of a reed pipe. Volodya is eyeing the rows of trees that stream by in the window. The terminal station, Lev Tolstoy street. A wooden fence. An elderly man wearing PJs and a straw hat staring into the distance is trying to make somebody out. Volodya walks right past him. The old man's name is Uncle Andrey, and he's waiting for an ambulance. His wife has once again suffered a heart attack.

Volodya keeps going. An alleyway. A gaggle of boys is playing soccer. A very obese boy is their goalkeeper. Let's see; who is their midfielder?

The girls, Rita and Sasha, are playing badminton. Their movements are smooth and fluid. The shuttlecock swims in the air.

Volodya, Volodya, the girls scream as he approaches.

*translated by Alex Cigale*

# Tony + Lyuda = Love

They met during the very height of the Cold War, and got married after the Soviet Union collapsed.

He picks her up at Kennedy Airport and drives her through the recently re-opened Midtown Tunnel. She didn't have time to exchange her rubles for dollars and is nervous about it, so that she doesn't even notice the grand scapes flying past the cab's window. Tony is looking at her in the cab's rearview mirror and can't get enough of her: bags under her eyes, her hair disheveled, but there's a certain, god dammit, je ne sais quoi that this monkey-of-a-life has yet to pick out from the angel cake and stick inside its hairy jowls. She was telling him about the changes taking place in Russia (he first thought she had said "in Prussia," but over dinner he understood that he had misheard her); he told her all about the Knicks.

It should be said that, at the historical juncture being described, the attitudes of Americans toward Russia contained a great deal of mistrust. It's no great mystery why: our countries were, at that time, issuing the most threatening decrees and ultimatums, and periodically even rattling their sabers: McNamara, the Cuban Missile Crisis, the square dances at the UN. And he's unshaven, but with his taxi driver's cap on, carries himself with genuine dignity: and this here is the United Nations, this in the past was a neighborhood of slaughterhouses, this river is called precisely that, the East River, it is both navigable and a fishery, but it is by no means Missouri, no, not the Missouri. He reminded Lyuda very much of her ex-husband, an informant type, with whom she had gotten engaged during their sophomore year at MGU, but they hadn't proved to be compatible: he drank and snooped around quite a bit. So here she is, having fallen for Tony, like some sort of seventh grader, God's own truth, for the married shop teacher, Oleg Grigorievich. They, Tony and comrade Lyudmila Butorenkov, had agreed to get together for supper. And among Americans, it should be noted, it is customary to get down on the carpet and suck the woman's titty only after the third supper. I know what I'm talking about; all my women-friends are either American or Canadian. There have been some Mexicans among them, but less often, and they are more impulsive in their urges, so that things sometimes don't even get to a third supper. And the thing is, Lyudmila and Tony didn't have much time, I'm sure you understand, for such extended preliminaries: in two days, she would have to return home to Leningrad; that's what Saint Petersburg was called under the Bolsheviks. And her manner of speech, I'm sure you understand, was more British than American. So he's telling her about boxing and baseball and puts his arm around her waist. She looks deep into his eyes, lets him kiss her. And they head off to her room. She starts to undress, right before him. He turns away, and she tells him: don't turn away, taxi driver! Look at me, a blindingly beautiful fair-skinned Russian woman abroad! Very soon, I'll let you do quite a lot to me, you'll see. And Tony's batting his eyes and doesn't understand a thing. She started pressing him: so you're gonna do it? He melded with her, breathing deeply, like a fish. She started speaking to him in Polish then for some reason, and she was wearing some very handsome, understated shoes and a tiny hat with a veil. That's all. And so he was perturbed. Really hot and bothered. He even scraped the skin off his fingers, the window looked onto Lexington Avenue—that's how much this all rattled him.

Several decades passed, like the night passes after a meal at an Indian restaurant: with complementary burping, you shouldn't have had all that sweet yogurt to go with the chicken (more than not likely, they just slaughtered the pigeon from the fire escape and stuffed it in the pot, end of story). Tony had long ago left his wife. Waited the entire time for comrade Butorenkov to arrive, hadn't forgot her appeal. And she did come after all, patience is a virtue, and then already with the rank of lieutenant colonel, a rare thing for a dame, but not unheard of, perhaps, perhaps a woman can be under a colonel! Old contacts, so much water under the bridge, a limited liability company, the ass. gen. director, they tore him a new one for flying so high over other people's coops, you never know, they might be someone.

They meet up. They sit there; in the meantime, he'd learned some Russian, just because. . . An awkward silence.

And suddenly, it all started off with a loud hiss and ended in a bang. No, not that, not terrorists, just some sort of equipment blew in the boiler room. They both got a real scare.

Tony and Lyuda are living in Florida now. It's the grand opening of their second café, the plastic pennants are flapping in the wind, he loves her madly and without measure. Carries her in his arms, naked, to the bedroom and back, to the bedroom and back, and often, and she's over sixty already. She reads Pasternak and Akhmatova to him, and more contemporary authors. . . But more about that after the espresso, maestro!

*translated by Alex Cigale*

# The Dead Wave

"No, but really, to argue with the claim that in the twentieth century economic information occupies a place equal to military and diplomatic information is difficult," our host was saying. He was a good-natured, rotund man in a silk turquoise robe with tassels. He was standing, short legs spread, in the center of the living room and puffing on an aromatic Cuban cigar. I was up to my neck in love with his twenty-year-old daughter, but did my best to conceal my feelings from her. She sat pouting by the fire. Her cheeks were ablaze. I decided to engage her in a conversation.

"Did you know, Klavdia," I began, clearing my throat, "that the writer Lev Veniaminovich Nikulin, who, incidentally, comes from your hometown Zhitomir, calls Lenin "The Helmsman" almost on the very first page of his novel *The Dead Wave*?

"Is that right?" the girl came alive. "Well, yesterday I saw a dead body in the courtyard."

"You're such a liar, Klavdia," I scolded. I was annoyed that the object of my affections was again changing the topic of conversation to the meaningless.

"But it's true. He was half-decomposed already, and smelled awful. There were worms crawling around in his testicles, and something had managed to gnaw off one of his buttocks."

"Klavdia!" her father shouted. "It's not proper for girls to talk of such things."

"Maybe not for virgins. . ." Klavdia smiled thinly.

Her words upset me. I had been under the impression that Klavdia was chaste.

"Klavdia!" again the host's voice rang out. "You can't possibly think that we are interested in. . ."

Suddenly there was a knock on the door, and the host hurried to welcome the final guest. It was a man of about 26, pale-faced, blond, with a twinkle in his gray eyes. Klavdia nimbly leapt from her chair, threw herself at him and began kissing him. Just then my attention was drawn to one of the guests who had seemed to me a distant relative of the host. Until the arrival of the young man, he had been following Klavdia's father's story rather indifferently. However, as soon as the new guest had seated himself near Klavdia, the distant relative's face underwent a transformation. From his mouth there emerged a shiny black box the length of three fingers, the width of one finger, and the depth of half a finger; he began to let out purplish-green and bright red sparks; foam spurt out of his ears and his legs stretched themselves around the young man's torso; three wings grew from his back, his head somehow detached itself from his neck and began to spin rapidly, and his body turned smoky. Without thinking, I bolted from the room. And not a minute too soon. For it was the devil. And not just any old opera devil in a leotard and fringes but the actual devil, the focal point of Absolute Evil, the Spirit of Destruction, the concentration of World Chaos and Negativity.

He had arrived to see the father of the object of my desire, since he had long been pursuing the young man who appeared last. The young man was a great actor, and thus, the rival of the devil, who, incidentally, could in no way be a distant relative of the host. And it was through the devil's incitement that Klavdia began the conversation about the corpse allegedly seen by her the night before the ill-fated evening.

Three days later, I was again at a party at Klavdia's father's house. No one mentioned the unpleasant episode. Klavdia was beguiling as always. Her father entertained us again with various stories of international industrial espionage. And only the

charred corpse of the young actor, sitting dead in the same arm-
chair where three days ago had sat the Spirit of Destruction, reminded us of the tragic event.

"Klavdia," I addressed the girl, still hoping to win her over.

"Yes," she replied coldly.

"Did you know, Klavdia, that the father of your fellow-
countryman Lev Veniaminovich Nikulin was a prominent figure
in the theater?"

"Like the late Stanislav?" she turned towards the charred actor.

And suddenly it dawned on me: it was the way she swayed to
and fro, the rustling of her light dress, the smell of sweat emanat-
ing from her armpits, and the suspicion with which she looked at
me sideways and bit her lower lip, and again and again looked
around at Stanislav, and the turquoise of her father's robe, and
Dylan's hoarse voice singing about how man gave names to all
the animals many years ago, and the song's unexpected end-
ing where something crawling disappeared among trees by
a lake—all this unequivocally pointed to the fact that no matter
how hard I'd try to charm Klavdia with my stories from writers'
lives, no matter how frequently I visited her house, and no matter what kinds of fine wines her father would serve. . .

*translated by Lydia Bryans and the author*

# Status Quo

Once down on the ashy beach Lida glanced about prudishly, pulled off her diminutive top, introducing two pale breakfast rolls, 50c apiece, turned this way and that, and at last managed to inflame a handsome vacationer called Tzvetan. Tzvetan offered Greek perfume, Fernandel classics, vigorously narrated sunsets—and waited.

Lida also waited. She buried a lover last winter—he was felled by a drunk driver—and she was conflicted: Should it be now, or a bit later?

One night, when Tzvetan had waited long enough, and *it* happened, a red-faced Greek in a pristine undershirt made them coffee ground with sugar powder and whistled something that sounded like Sirtaki, reggae mix.

Then they left the island and wandered. On the night train from Venice to Vienna Lida noted that Tzvetan didn't make a habit of changing his shorts and thought to voice her opinion on the matter. Her last guy had always kept himself extra clean.

"Had is key," said Tzvetan. "Probably not so worried about it now."

"Idiot," retorted Lida.

When the iron curtain came down Lida went to Madrid to make money. She sang Gorbachev chastushkas in the subway, then joined a band of midgets from Dushanbe, juggled and made do. Her late lover picked her up in the Retiro Park by the equestrian Alfonso XII. He was a black guy with a bit of Russian.

"Remember, stinker: once you tried black, there's no going back," Lida told Tzvetan, still feeling a bit sore.

"Something wrong?" asked Tzvetan going down the escalator.

"It's in your pants," said Lida when they got to the hotel. "You probably want to do laundry at some point."

"After I smoke," promised Tzvetan, capitulating for the moment. He worked for the railroad and he'd been all over Europe for half price. Seeing the world was more important to him than smelling like a Bulgarian rose. So he told her:

"Seeing the world is more important to me, baby, than smelling like a Moscow lily."

"Stick that baby. . ." snapped the young lady.

From the hotel she called her sister in Saratov. She called her whenever they got to a new place.

"An'ka! You little bitch! What's buggin', pisshead? You'll shit yourself when you see the getups here! Fuckin' A!"

Lida was seriously starting to get on his nerves. Now this laundry business. Maybe he's not crazy about her shorts either. Clean, dirty, whatever—he's just not into it. All the ruffles and whatnots—fuckin' A! And the prepositions are all wrong, not like in Bulgarian. Why can't she just piss out?

Tzvetan looked down from the balcony. Money will be all gone before the next town. He thought about the wife he left behind in Sofia. She went crazy—the doctors were perfectly useless—and he decided to leave her. Not right away, though. At first he tried to look after her. She called herself Hitler's bride, not Eva Braun, but another one, younger and virtually unknown to historians. "He wanted to give me Poland, but I refused like a little idiot. Now it's too late!" she cried, wrestling with the orderlies. Tzvetan couldn't bear it, and so he left. . . What if she really was Hitler's lover? Let's see—they shot the Führer in Milan, 1948. Kristina was born in '49. Doesn't quite work out, mathematically, does it?.. But then there are such things as prenatal attachments, womb crushes, as it were. What do we do with those? Ignore them? Christ, I must be going mad too. . . She's still in there, clacking away. But what if this isn't Vienna, and they're already in Prague, partying like the nouveau Czechs and strolling through the Old Town? And a shriveled man in a cream-colored coat comes down from the hills across the river, and he says bleakly: It's all over. And the people below call out to him: What is? What's over? And he tells them: Are you deaf? I'm telling you—all of it.

An endless tale. . . turning on itself like the Greek dance Sirtaki. . . History that bears no fruit. A tale of a Russian girl who steals money from a Bulgarian man, while he goes out to smoke on the balcony. And while she washes her underwear he restores the status quo.

*translated by Sergey Levchin*

# Wish You Were Here:
# A Few Postcards from New York

## 1

You arrive in an unfamiliar city. Of course, it's not complete-ly unfamiliar: you've heard about it, read something, seen a few postcards, flipped through a magazine called America.

Which means, you arrive in a not-completely-unfami-liar city.

Before the punks came along with their multicolored roost-er mohawks and leather jackets, you remember being a kid and catching sight of respectable-looking older women in their soft blue chignons and their lit cigarettes all done up in bright lip-stick. These were tourists from the Bronx or Arizona, spilling out of their tour buses in a thick-thighed herd in front of the Black Sea Hotel. Proto-punks is what they were. Like some sort of cockatoos, but with chewing gum and ballpoint pens—which you begged for shamelessly, forgetting about Pioneer's pride.

Once upon a time, Lorca arrived in New York and headed to Harlem to hear jazz. Mayakovsky arrived and telephoned Burliuk. And Ilf and Petrov arrived and met Hemingway. And you—you arrived and what? Nothing. The famous are always be-ing led around: to meet so and so, give a talk at such and such. But nobody leads the un-famous anywhere. The un-famous must lead himself. And is often led astray. (Papa could never navigate the subway system and that's why he was always getting mad at everybody.)

In Moscow—another city not your own—during winter va-cation everything was opposite. You opened the curtains in your hotel room and instead of a savings bank and a sausage shop, outside your window the arrangement was different. You become aware of the different when something familiar (let's say, a gesture) precedes something unfamiliar (let's say, a view). You step across that threshold and everything is different: the temperature, the trolley number. And the milk you drink before you go to bed is from a weird-sounding dairy. You want to remember a strange city down to the finest details because you know you'll never live there. But the city where you'll settle—well, you'll still have time to capture all the minor details, so what's the rush? Empire State Building? There's always time. Yeah—and you still haven't been.

Before your arrival, and for a period after, the not-completely-unfamiliar city is for you the sum of all the references you've come across. In due time they materialize, reality introduces its corrections, but the aftertaste of the reference remains. Lennon yelling "Down in the Village!" on his album *Some Time in New York City* ceases to be a misinterpreted appeal for the back-to-nature movement, and becomes— after your arrival—what it was for the songwriter: a reference to a neighborhood in lower Manhattan. And it was there, too, in the Village, that another reference wandered: Salinger's Holden Caulfield.

This referential perception of the city is a particular example of a tourist's frame of mind. The city you arrive in is no city of supermarkets and bank lines, but the city of Sister Carrie and the heroes of O. Henry. And Central Park is not the locus of sleeping bums and mischievous teenagers, but the setting for Woody Allen's lovestruck heroes in *Manhattan* strolling through, and for Holden, too, trying melancholically to figure out where the ducks go in the winter when the pond freezes over.

"Over there is the pond where Holden. . ." the female carriage driver said to you during your midnight ride through Central Park in that summer of '78. "And there"—she pointed to a tall building on the West Side—"is the Dakota, where Lennon lives, and where they shot the movie *Rosemary's Baby*."

Two years later Mark David Chapman left his dog-eared copy of *The Catcher in the Rye* on the wet sidewalk near the entrance to the Dakota. Two references canceling out each other, merging gruesomely into one. And so the city forever lost the aftertaste of someone else's lines, became a city unencumbered by quotation marks, became yours.

A city whose misfortunes were your own, no longer borrowed from elsewhere.

## 2

That first job: Doubleday Publishing House. You packed books, manuscripts. The former you sent out to reviewers; the latter, to authors, along with a note: "Thanks, but no thanks," or: "Not badly written. Thanks, but no thanks."

Your first thrills: the Wednesday book sale for employees. Hardcopies, twenty-five cents. Paperbacks, a dime.

Those first encounters: Jackie O in the hallway. No longer young but still quite something. She was an editor there. At the cafeteria, you tucked in line behind a frumpy old man with Goncharov-like sideburns. Turned out to be Asimov. That was nice, too.

During lunch you hurried to the peep show. Sticky floor, plastic cocks, vaginas of fantastical proportions, the smell of bleach and sperm. Big fellows in grey suits flipping through the picture magazines, then walking into private booths and spraying their elderly seed to the whir of the projector. On the cheap (you could settle in for three cycles at twenty-five cents a pop) and with no frills (it's still coming out, but it's time to exit).

Then a girl came along. Now there were lunches together. Kisses, sandwiches. Calling the fat pigeons near the library "stoners" since in the park nearby you could score anything the heart desired; sometimes, the pigeons also stumbled onto a fix.

One day you scored something, too. Spent the entire day working with your head in the clouds.

You got acquainted during the blackout. The heat that day was 100 degrees, and Con Ed went apeshit.

## 3

You sat in the cool movie theater on 42nd & 7th and struggled to grasp the plot of *Pop My Cherry, Dirty Harry*. You'd arrived late: you'd lingered at the entrance for about five minutes, couldn't work up the nerve to buy a ticket from the lady at the window with the sign saying "air-conditioned." Usually there was a fat man with a shaved head in a leather coat, drowning in his own corpulence, or a runty black teenager who sat at the window and now, all of a sudden—a respectable, middle-aged woman.

A Puerto Rican guy with a document case under his arm sped things up. The man hurried on by and stopped for a second. Then he chirped up like a boy scout, trying to provoke the woman (it was clear he wasn't going into the theater):

"They fucking in there, grandma?"

"Oh, they're fucking alright, sonny boy!" the old woman shot back, and she naughtily smacked her lips.

The young Puerto Rican let out a laugh and ran on further and you took a confident step closer to the window and handed the woman four dollars.

You sat somewhere in the middle—equidistant from the back rows, where young couples helped each other empathize with the characters on screen, and from the front, where retirement-aged folk managed as best they could to please themselves. You learned this simple tactic—choosing a good seat—easily, since in your first six months in New York, you watched nothing but porn flicks.

All of a sudden the moaning of the writhing actresses became drawn out, then turned into a retching sound, as if at the worst possible moment they had decided to vomit into each other's mouths. The screen went dark but they didn't turn on the lights in the theater, and the howls of fire truck sirens penetrated from the street. For a second you thought war had broken out.

A minute later, in line at the ticket window, you calmed down, hearing the words "blackout"—which was indistinguishable to your ears from "lights out." "Lights out" was a phrase you were familiar with, and "blackout," judging from it all, was something semantically close. And the old woman at the ticket window wouldn't be handing out tickets to anybody who wanted to finish watching the love story of Harry the San Francisco biker and three nudist nurses, if war had just broken out!

The uproar on the street was out of the ordinary. The crash of breaking glass. Somewhere in the distance a hot dog cart was burning. Shouts of "Loose joints, check 'em out" were louder than usual. People in pairs and by themselves ran across the street with boxes of different dimensions, from which one could deduce: television, small washing machine, lamp, vacuum cleaner. At least the criminal element and temporary proponents of free domestic wares believed that electricity would return and life would go back to normal.

A week later the newspapers compared the damage caused in the city on those days with the damage resulting from the blackout of ten years prior. It turned out that ten years before, everything had been relatively calm, and you said to her, "Did everybody really live better, has humanity gone downhill since then?" And she said, "Yesterday is always a lot better than today, even when you're sleeping with the lights on." And she also said, "A bright future is the promise of the present minus electricity bills," and you thought, "She's crazy, but she's attractive."

You first noticed her in the subway. It was hot in there, like on the street, but at least the subway had lights.

## 4

Your private life for the most part took place at the movies. At first you groped each other in alleyways, and you already had your hand under her skirt, rounding the bases, when she told you this was childish, there was no way you'd ever fuck. That word grated on you. Back home, where you were from, they didn't speak like that. People said, make it, or screw. The last one was vulgar, but you preferred vulgarity to crudeness. Fucking was crude. But you got used to her crudeness. And you got used to her casual ways. But with no car and the folks at home, what could you do?

It was a no-go at *Star Wars* because of the noisy special effects and the screeching children. Neither one was conducive. At the Waverly, watching Dylan's *Renaldo and Clara*, the seats were too uncomfortable and the film was impossible to make sense of—go figure out who's Renaldo, who's Clara. And finally, oh, the desired moment, at the Bleecker Street Cinema, practically on her haunches, she nearly drove you through the roof. It was at a screening of *The Conformist*, and you silently came in a popcorn bucket during the famous forest scene. You were surprised at the theatricality of that scene, it was almost operatic. At the falafel place across the street later you played it out for her. "Damn!" She liked your telling of it but she wasn't happy she'd missed so much. "Didn't you enjoy yourself?" "How should I put it?" she answered, with a vague gesture. "It's somehow more democratic. . . lying down." "Lying down you need a bed," you said. "Can we scrape together rent?" She repeated the same gesture.

You spent a long time looking for an apartment. Everything was expensive. She didn't care for Brooklyn. "To stay in Brooklyn is to stay an immigrant forever," she said. You found an agent in Jackson Heights, you thought you were smart but he stuck you with a lemon: he rented you a place with poor light (although, when you'd gone to look at it, it had seemed so bright), more expensive than you'd planned, and on top of everything, it was above a diner. The smoke from the hamburgers got in the way of watching the TV, the windows looked out onto nowhere. Literally nowhere: at the new place, after sex on top of the suitcases, on the third attempt you were able to open the window and. . . you couldn't see anything. In front of your eyes was solid brick, and you really needed a drink.

*translated by Ross Ufberg*

# Bobby the Loon

At this point no one could say for certain how former town idiot, food-and-drink specialist Boris O. Perelmutter made his way to New York City. Some said that in the far-off eighty blank he came with a delegation, on some sort of exchange, and that on their last day in the Big Apple he asked for political asylum. Maybe. Others said that he was a decent bassist, and that he got a part-time gig at a little jazz club on Hudson St.; that he bewitched the proprietress, a hot little Filipina named Maria, and got himself a green card that way. Another maybe.

Whichever way it happened, the first thing he did when he got here was to call me. We had been schoolmates, but were never friendly, and I was surprised to hear his voice on the other end of the line. Frankly, it bothered me. My recollections of this person were far from warm. In school he was cocky with us and brash with the teachers; insufferably vain, he was prone to bouts of unmotivated rage, often spilling over into violence. His arrogance and insolence were boundless. For whatever reason it made him popular with some of the girls. This irritated me to no end. One of these girls even promised to show him something for three rubles, but Boris would only give two. She wouldn't come down. That day, over lunch break, he shoved her against the coat rack and got to see whatever it was he wanted free of charge. Needless to say, the girl was scared shitless. After that we started calling him Bobby the Loon.

In Biology, while the rest of us dutifully copied gymnosperms in cross-section into our notebooks, Bobby communed with the Lord in a loud whisper. "O Lord," prayed Bobby, "just give me death, or immortality, or something along those lines; don't just sit there in silence, pretending I don't exist. Lord, I exist." The Lord either pretended, or didn't pretend, or I don't know what.

Bobby got kicked out in our junior year after Ms. Gorelik, a young woman who taught Russian, read out his free-form essay at the teachers' meeting. The essay was titled "My One True Love." Bobby's literary sensation was still wildly popular by the time we were graduating. Multiple hand-written copies were in circulation, and by some miracle I had kept one with me, even to this day. I will reproduce it here verbatim and in full, largely because I fear that my cursory account of Bobby's early years will fail to produce a true impression of this, mildly put, peculiar personality.

*My One True Love*

*My first love was a hot little bitch; she had a face of rare beauty, full, sensuous lips and a spry ass. Whenever she sensed a deficiency between her legs she promptly pulled off her panties, which swarmed with pink bunnies and other such critters, and pressing herself close to me whispered, "Kiss me, Bobbikins." I loved her on average once every two days, but she always wanted more, more.*

*One time, when our parents went to a party, and she had recently turned eight, she made me drink a full glass of her shimmering, fragrant urine. "This will make it harder," she explained.*

*She insists that this summer we formalize our engagement. I tried to explain to her that Jews look down on marriages between brothers and sisters before the age of 11, but she would have none of it. My baby goes by Baby Rosie. Now I will describe her inner world: it is warm, moist, mellifluous. There, I've described it.*

How is that? Now you understand what sort of lunatic this was. The "essay" was read all over town; some genius even tried setting it to music. Three days after the teachers' conference Bobby was thrown out with a scandal; he proclaimed himself alternately samizdat martyr or hapless victim of anti-Semitism. He strolled up and down the boulevard in his worn corduroy bells, tilting his head unnaturally, swinging his long arms, and yelled out at strangers, "What now? Any other questions? That's right. You thought you were the only one! What?" After that his "fame" spread beyond our school and he became known all over town as a real-life maniac.

I, for one, knew perfectly well that there was no sister. Bobby was the only child of fairly well-off parents: his father was a big shot at something called MariTrade & Trans, and his mother was heiress to a cash-and-carry. Bobby got everything he asked for; this irritated me even further, and Bobby knew it well.

By now it should be clear to the reader why I wavered not little before agreeing to meet him after all this time. Finally, among my various arguments contra, I had to admit the following facts: Bobby is alone in a strange land. If he called me it means that there is really nobody else. I have a moral obligation to help another human being, just like somebody else had helped me in the day before I was systems analyst at Merrill Lynch. And besides, I pleaded with myself, he's not the same Bobby anymore.

I met him in the city, at the Café Orlin on St. Mark's. He had certainly changed, at least in appearance: he'd gained some weight, his hair had gone gray around his temples, and missing elsewhere. Only his eyes had retained the same look of languid insolence. I ordered two cappuccinos. Sitting back in my chair I asked him casually what he had been up to over the years, hoping to avert a similar question in the other direction. I didn't want to talk about my work (my personal life isn't really worth talking about) because I don't like bragging; and I would have to brag: I was recently promoted to project manager, head of IT. There was no point in parading my successes before the newly arrived and presumably struggling. Especially if the parade was likely to culminate in a timid request for a loan or some help finding work.

Within two minutes I realized that my strategy had misfired horribly. It would have been far better to talk about myself. Taking a thick slurp of his cappuccino, Bobby launched into a tale of his wife, whom he had apparently left shortly before getting out of the country. To hear him, she was a perfect angel, sans wings, and he was beating himself up over his indiscretion. I was getting ready to start patting him on the back and offering my condolences—though I didn't yet know in what words—perhaps even suggesting we trade our cappuccinos for something a bit stiffer; but just then Bobby decided to share with me a couple of scenes from his conjugal life with what I could only describe as pathological frankness. Like I said, my conversation strategy was starting to backfire. . . On the other hand, what else are two people supposed to talk about when they haven't seen each other for the last fifteen years? The past is all they have. . .

"My wife was a real beauty," intoned Bobby in his hoarse, bleating voice, "intelligent, olive skin, dark areolas, her feces were especially pungent. A splendid cook. And so neat! She changed her pants three times a day. Shall I tell you? Every time she farted she'd go and stick a daisy up her ass. Flowers needs nourishment too, am I right? How could I ever walk out on a girl like that?"

I wanted very much to change the subject. "Listen," I said, "how did you end up here, anyway? As far as I remember you weren't planning on going anywhere." He pretended not to hear me and went on.

"I loved her a lot. A lot. Whatever I could get my hands on I stuck it up her cunt. Tickled her with my cock. Pissed on her belly. Read poetry. She was working as a guide for Intourist, and I was going to night school for food management; during the day I was fixing kerosene burners in the market—dad got pinched by the ass then, so we had to make do. One summer day I came home and threw myself on top of Vika (this was my wife's sister) with a knife in my hand, and I killed her accidentally. What was I supposed to do? My baby was coming home in half an hour and there was a corpse in the middle of the room. Laura didn't like to get upset (that was her name—Laura, Loreley, my little laundromat), I had to act fast. I dragged the corpse under the bed, and licked up all the blood from the rug. I still had about a quarter of an hour left, so I climbed under the bed with Vika and we made love. 'Vika, Vika, do you love me, even a little bit?' I queried, working her stiffening legs.

"That's when Laura came through the door. 'Bobby, yoo-hoo!' she cried and started changing her pants—that's just how she was. I stuck my head out from under the bed and crawled toward my wife, clowning about and stretching out my tongue toward her thick calves. She patted my member and understood everything instantly; she hit me hard in the face and then started tearing out my hair. She just lost her shit. I had blood pouring out of my nose, but it didn't matter. I pulled her pants over her head and wrestled her to the ground; I was licking her clit and at the same time sniffing the daisy that was poking out of her ass.

"'She loves me, she loves me not,' I tried to make out.

"After a hearty breakfast the next morning I was getting ready for work, as usual. Laura was pulling on a new pair of pants and trying to talk to Vika. 'Why, oh why did I marry this animal?' she kept saying. But Vika didn't like meddling in our affairs, so she basically kept quiet. . ."

"Listen, here!" I protested, "You told me you had killed this Vika! I don't get it!"

"Maybe you should just keep your mouth shut, then you'd get it," snapped Bobby unexpectedly.

"No, you tell me everything straight: you stabbed your sister-in-law, then you had sex with the corpse, right? The next morning she and your wife are having a nice old chat—what is this about, anyway?"

"Idiot!" Bobby was getting seriously mad. "You and your shitty America. Do they rot your brains here on purpose?"

"Why don't you watch your language," I said, still trying to keep calm. "What's America have to do with anything?"

"Nothing. You're right. You were already a total dumbass back in school," said Bobby, somewhat quietly, and suddenly he jumped up and lunged at me.

I wasn't especially crazy about any of it, but I had no intention of getting into a fight: Bobby was a full head taller than me. I snatched up my coat, threw some money on the table and ran out of the café, cursing my kindness and my weakness.

What in the world did I agree to meet him for? He hadn't changed a bit, time or no time—Bobby was the same goddam psycho he was in high school. What did I care about his wife's nuanced shit, or what she had growing out of her ass? Suppose he just made up the whole thing, beginning to end—why did I have to hear about it? Did he want to shock me? Is it some sort of inferiority complex with all the recent arrivals: they don't like our smug looks, our patronizing gestures... Is that why Bobby wanted to knock me off-balance with his moronic exploits? And if they are not made-up? Why, then, did he react so violently to my question? He even tried to hit me...

Sadly, I will never have answers to these questions. My meeting with Bobby proved to be the last. Half a year later I discovered by accident that Boris Perelmutter killed himself by jumping from a 7th story balcony of a building across from the Bronx Zoo. His neighbors reported that he had stood for a long time on the balcony, waving his arms in the freezing air; someone even proposed that he was exercising. He was shouting and calling someone "indifferent" or "inhuman"—he wanted his unseen opponent to get it once and for all that he—was; the others, the

thick-headed bastards were not, but he was, he existed supreme-
ly! Some of the tenants had gathered below and told him to cut
the crap and let people sleep. This was some time after midnight.
Bobby roared with laughter like a complete maniac, then he leapt
over the railing. A second later he hit the sidewalk. He died in the
hospital without regaining consciousness.

*translated by Sergey Levchin*

# some folks call it paranoia

theyre on to me he blurted out but it came out sounding like theyre under me and she heard theyll run to me huh? she asked looking in the mirror dolling herself up a fashionista so pale lovely a little tired so nice so pale he repeated it who she asked turning to him a little tired a bit sad i don't know he answered but theyre on to me they follow me just dont say stupid things you remind me of those crazies on tv your complete unconcern he started to get excited your supreme confidence that everything will turn out exactly as you want that everything that happens somehow wont touch you wont concern you affect you on the dressing table in front of her were little bottles jars boxes gucci lancôme chanel passion and a whole regiment of gleaming lipsticks in full regalia she didnt like makeup i am not a canvas for the old masters from revlon and loreal i am a woman i dont want to hide my real face she said and kept buying everything she could get her hands on anyway and hid it hid it from him what for he asked when he found them well why do you have all those ties you know some of them you havent worn even once and you buy and buy and buy them you gave me half of them oh you dont say that means its all my fault yet again nobody is accusing you of anything i thought you always approved of my choices and what exactly was i supposed to say what a revolting color take away this abomination or nobody has worn wide ties for the past year and a half? and they burst out laughing she clung to him kissed him so who whos on to you my silly goose who i dont know he sighed but i cant shake the feeling someone is always watching me when I take a taxi to work in business meetings at the bar with friends

after work and at home and even when we are making love supposedly alone supposedly behind closed doors supposedly poor
thing my poor thing youre just burned out we really need a vacation we really must have a vacation soon how long can you let
them run you into the ground when well when well when did they
promise to give you a vacation on christmas? on thanksgiving? on
memorial day? on labor day? they keep promising and promising
but memorial day comes labor day passes thanksgiving is coming
up and we are only a stones throw from christmas and you still
work and work if you only knew how I hate it your damned work
you have bags under your eyes from it you have this general list-
lessness from it even though you drink a ton of coffee everybody
drinks decaf but you drink caf your hair has started to fall out
what do you mean no heres a mirror look for yourself for yourself
there and there and there and what is that? well? and this belly
when did you last get to the gym well when? the hair and the belly
arent from work he tried to object she sat on his lap stroking his
indeed rather prematurely chubby belly the belly and the hair
loss are from age ridiculous dont be ridiculous she switched to
a whisper: at thirty-two years of age [inaudible] a man should not
have [inaudible] work allows us to live work allows us to pay off
an apartment in one of the toniest parts of town work allows us
to [inaudible] work keeps us from having sex work will force me
to cheat on you someday you will mark my words how many well
how many times in the past three months have we had sex well
cmon tell me how many she started to unzip his fly maybe six or
seven times he said uncertainly three she said and slowly started
to give him a massage thats wrong it cant be just three he said
three she said i wrote down the dates duration positions i wrote
down everything well arent you a regular masters and johnson
he cracked agh just not now stop do you hear she continued to
amuse herself why why not now today is saturday if not now then
when? tell me when? no matter when i start you are always like

not now and how is now any worse than later i am telling you i cannot get rid of this feeling of persecution even now even now? yes right now! these are just excuses these are all just your excuses and these excuses of yours no longer work these are not excuses yes excuses no youre wrong yes excuses no yes no yes no yes theyre excuses no theyre not stop it right now i will not stop yes you will excuses not excuses no yes no yes not excuses theyre watching me theyre watching me watching me i dont know who I know that they are watching watching watching day and night theyre watching me never stopping watching me excuses excuses youre just avoiding sex i cant when they are watching I am not an exhibitionist for gods sake he said and zipped up his fly but do you know who is watching you she asked and abruptly got off his lap i dont know of course you do i have no idea he answered oh yes you do she said who he asked you know who she shouted and in one fell swoop knocked off the little table all her little flasks jars boxes flasks jars bottles boxes they jumped off rained down bounced around on the floor [at this point the recording is interrupted].

They were in a fight for a week. After that they made up. Shortly after we received and transcribed the video recording of her quarrel with her husband, one of our colleagues established contact with her. Based on preliminary data, the recruitment is going well. She has agreed to work with us, but money, according to her, holds no interest for her.

*translated by Kerry Philben*

# De Kooning

Not long before his divorce from Veronika Sergeevna Petr Andreevich plunged into abstractions. This meant turning his rifle onto a line of color tubes, evenly spaced and laid out before a stretch of canvas tacked to the side of a two-car garage (burgundy BMW of his better half, and his own vaguely-hued Capri). The tubes exploded, shooting globs of paint onto the canvas and hypostasizing there in a variety of abstract forms: e.g., a cloud formation resembling the rape of the Sabine women; or knotted and gnarled grapevines that also passed for a row of twisting beauties; or even blood-colored hoop skirts that made your head spin. Petr Andreevich had been known to favor the visual arts and even sculpted lightly on weekends, but the prospect of a bachelor's existence now prompted him to take up the brush—i.e., rifle—and redraw the fluid boundaries between art and life. Wife as model, as object of desire, deprived of a third dimension, but still in full possession of shopping bags and beauty aids—an abstract wife à la de Kooning, sullen and seldom willing—came to dominate his entire process. After a shooting session Petr Andreevich typically removed the canvas to the shed, where he continued his work—sometimes for weeks on end—painstakingly imposing order (and thus meaning) upon the chaos wrought through actionist practices, which he had dubbed art-art (i.e., artillery art), whether in jest or in earnest, I don't know.

Veronika Sergeevna had long resolved to quit smoking. She would drop vulgar Parliaments for the Dunhill menthols, but close friend and yoga instructor Kimberly Bolik informed her over a frappuccino that menthol was even more harmful to the organism. And so it came that round-cheeked, big-toothed Veronika Sergeevna put out decisively her final cigarette in a Starbucks "garden"—because she had sworn she would but a year before, during a protracted coughing fit in the midst of a day spa, where she was shift manager. She had stopped loving her husband in the fall and let it be known. I don't love you, she said to Petr Andreevich with brutal frankness. Petr Andreevich stifled dejection and produced a humorous retort. He fished a frosty Carlsberg from the fridge, took a few sizable gulps and went out to shoot some tubes. This was a kind of art-art-therapy for him.

When lo and behold appears in the narrative a certain professor of immunology, of German extraction, en attendant a more powerful electron microscope. Whither he came (Wuppertal?) and what brought him to our shores (Lufthansa?) nobody can recall. But he managed to lure the whole world to his birthday shindig, pressed them on the first name basis, and promised to be the life of their next party. He feels an extraordinary influx of energy here in a new place and stands rocking back and forth on his rubber soles, smiling gallantly at his guests and whistling Rosina's aria from *The Barber of Seville*, while Claire and I are standing in the corner like poor relations, trying to reason whether it would be alright to have some more wine now or maybe some of those crackers with the foie gras, or is that going too far, or maybe ask the Frau to dance and twirl her all round the parlor and later whisper sweet nothings in her ear while they question that Habsburg Chap in the basement and whip him across his stubbly cheeks (with slippers, though it still hurts), and Petr Andreevich tells the prof's tearing (from boredom) brother of the time when Ronald Reagan presented him with a watch for saving the President's life—that's when he was interning with the secret service at the ballistics unit and Veronika Sergeevna was living in Georgetown with her mother, and this is how they met, and he asked her on the first date who was her favorite film director, only seriously, and she was embarrassed, but in the end came out okay with Billy Wilder. Early stuff.

Now, the old unfurl their tales before the young, because the young must find it all terribly interesting, while in reality they find it perfectly indifferent. You talk about yourself because it's really about life, and about them—but it isn't about them, it's about you. It's nothing to them. They will nod, but every nod of theirs is a great yawn suppressed, believe me. Your life has passed, and there is nothing to be had from it, not just because it was another place, now gone, but also because it was another time, now also gone. The place has changed and the time is passed. While you, as a function of both variables, are similarly absent, or altered, and superfluous in this time or this place. Especially because you showed up sporting what thinking people haven't worn in ages. The collar is wrong, should be brighter and more green. Nobody under thirty-five would even think of putting on a second-chin, ditto the retro bags under the eyes. And the melancholy, the fatigue, the disappointment.

She isn't bad, that Frau.

Next weekend chez Petr Andreevich. He'll bring out Reagan's watch like he always does. But Veronika Sergeevna has quit smoking and become irritable; she demands to be squeezed when she's dancing. I'm happy to oblige, but only with Petr Andreevich's kind permission. That's just a matter of principle. Then came the abstractions.

We see a fountain, fishes swimming in the pool, a woman with a stroller sits on a bench, reading *Army of One*, that's the one about a spy. Wondrous: Petr Andreevich shot some tubes by his garage and out came mama with her book, and me six months old, our park with the fountain and the bicyclist in black. Or is that a boy with a dripping eye whizzing about on a scooter? Can't tell. But still very pretty and true to life.

Some scoundrel is spanking his Hungarian wife and grunting, "There! And there! And there's more of that there!" How is it the earth still bears his kind upon her crooked green back? And the neighbors turning a blind eye to the tube.

A pretty girl got all dolled up, flowers in hand, waiting for her fiancée. Here comes a frightful imp, hobbling up—she wouldn't open to him at first, but dried up quickly enough and nolens volens hop and landed on his tail. He just peeped in a paper cup, if you know what I mean.

Petr Andreevich is accepting compliments with bemused modesty. The immunologist likes the pieces, so does Claire, though in the latter case it's more out of politeness. Her true opinions on abstract art are well known to me. Looks like it came out his ass one morning, she concluded bluntly outside the recent Max Wollenstein show in DC. She said it quietly, so that nobody else could hear.

Now this. Scoffing at contemporary art has become a commonplace, getting in line behind the new champions of mimesis and catharsis, pooh-poohing the mercurial rise of the Croatian performance artist, name escapes me, mustachioed, the one that was barking into a megaphone about globalization from the top of the Himalayas for like a whole month. Life isn't standing still, you know. Only yesterday one still felt safe making spurious connections between the pleasure afforded by Jeff Koons' sculptures circa '91 and the pleasure afforded to Jeff Koons by the Italian Cicciolina. Today those tender *fuck that cock! fuck that cock baby!* demand a more serious, interdisciplinary approach. *Bear and Policeman*—what's that really about? Deterritorialization? Insert amount? Sure it's funny. Is that it? *The Bespectacled Monkey* in the Patriarch's Ponds is also funny, but there's a concrete meaning there, a moral.

But where is the lady of the house? Veronika Sergeevna had dragged the professor's brother off to the garage to show him something, and they've been showing in there for the last 20 minutes. Could it be that she finally broke down and the two of them are having a private smoke? The professor's brother is still young and inexperienced; he is apt to blush fearfully when addressed by ladies. I think he's interested in Claire. He's been here for some two years, studying to be an ophthalmologist. He's the one that had intercepted the Habsburg Chap, trying to cross the border; it was a sheer accident too.

A woman abandoned is likened to earth that bears no fruit. And what about a man abandoned? Fruit that bears no earth? But where's it coming from, the fruit? How can it come about without the earth?

People vanish. Some are found, some are never looked for. People are also snatched by time. Here's a young attractive girl, but ah! she's already going gray in some unexpected places.

A devil in a white leotard strolls up and down the terrace, peddling eternal youth. One fool bought it. Another fool bought it. A third—seemingly intelligent—also bought it. Now he's sad: all his friends died, nobody left to call.

And another one: two drunks stop in the street, one tells the other, "You know what's the most important thing? The most important thing. . ." and off they go. And I'm left there, wondering what the most important thing is. I can't go after them, now can I?

*translated by Sergey Levchin*

# The Death of Samusis

Immediately after dinner, the rain began to fall. On the roof of the skyscraper opposite, four workers were tackling a supersized letter "A". On the street below, colorful pinpoints were dimming and then expanding—the passersby opening their umbrellas. He was standing at the window, clutching his heart. The head of his department exclaimed in passing: "Are we taking a little break now?" He grabbed onto the windowsill and his knees buckled. His coworkers surrounded him and someone ran over to the telephone. Cold drops of sweat erupted on his forehead. Once upon a time he dreamed: "I'll finish my course of studies, get married, and my wife will love me just for who I am."

He was now lying on the floor. Someone was unbuttoning the collar of his shirt. Once upon a time he dreamed: "My wife will be a homemaker." Someone slid their hand into his pocket and removed his wallet. His breathing became more rapid. Someone said: "He's having a heart attack. Where the hell is the damn doctor?" He wanted to object but the sounds emerging from his mouth would not coalesce into words. Some joker from Human Resources unzipped his pants and began massaging him. When people started admonishing the man, he explained: "I'm giving him shiatsu."

And so Samusis—for that was the name of the departed—died with an erection. For the final nine years of his life he had worked in a corporation where, from time to time, in one of the stalls in the men's restroom on his floor, the following inscription would appear: "Death to capitalism!"

"There you go—he thought to himself, flushing the toilet a day before his demise—a critique of the dominant order is possible only in places where the physical needs of people are met, where nature calls. On the john, we are all radicals."

The following day, he was already out of sorts from the morning on. Perhaps for this reason, when his son called and asked for money to buy umbrellas, he hurled a pile of insults at him, even calling him a good-for-nothing idiot, on whom being born and being educated was all wasted effort.

"One might think you were the one who gave birth to me, or educated me," Samusis the younger erupted before slamming down the phone receiver.

What we have here is a more or less standard beginning of a story—the death of the hero, the conflict preceding it, then the thoughts of one of the participants in the conflict are described, then the other participant, for example, takes a toke from a joint, and here one may already permit a succinct instance of stream of consciousness, a relaxation of the logical chains of causation, etc. However, we are pursuing here somewhat different aims, are we not? We can no longer be wowed by psychological realism, n'est-ce pas? And, truth be told, we already find modernism repulsive. (I've had the occasion to previously address in these pages my feelings about post-modernism and the new sentimentality.)

And so, the telephone conversation with his son left a particularly unpleasant sensation in Samusis the elder's mouth, but we will not here describe his subsequent thoughts and actions (all the more because in another four and a half hours he will no longer be among the living), but instead, let us jump in our thoughts to the year 1970, when Samusis the elder himself was not in the least a fool for rolling a crisp dollar bill into a short straw and, having previously chopped up the white substance on the surface of the mirror, pinching one of his nostrils with his index finger, and with the other nostril inhaling the aforementioned

powder through the same dollar straw to the sounds of his favorite song "Within You Without You" wafting from the single
working speaker of his decrepit old stereo. Have you jumped in
time with us? Very well then. And now, once again in thought
only, let us jump two and a half hours ahead, when Samusis the
elder, wearing only his tidy whities, is chasing through the corridor of the dormitory after a cackling brunette with a pretty blue
vein on her left temple. Then the brunette, having shut her eyes,
groans on the mangy carpet of her cramped room while Samusis
the elder, hiking up her mini-skirt, labors to issue Samusis the
younger, all the time snorting loudly while trying to throttle her
hips with both of his arms. And now (again in thought only) we
will jump another twenty some minutes into the future. Samusis
and the future mother of Samusis the younger are lying together
on the bed happily exhausted, sharing a cigarette and smiling at
each other.

And in another twenty three years, Samusis fought with his
son for some flimsy reason. Essentially, there was no reason at all
for it. Could it be that these measly 750 dollars where at the heart
of the matter? Simply a pool of mutual aggravation, accumulat-
ing over a period of many weeks, suddenly as though of its own,
spat up into a sizable quarrel. Though it should be noted that Samusis the younger was by nature a tactful youth and in his own
way loved his father. Literally five minutes after the phone call,
he was already repenting his rudeness and blaming himself and
himself only for the conflict with his father.

It bears repeating that May showers had always weighed
heavily on him with their feelings of melancholy, verging on
a familial species of anxiety. And now this stupid conversation!
Samusis the younger stood in the corner pinching his wispy sideburns. For some reason they were not buying his umbrellas, even
though business would otherwise be brisk on days like these. He
hadn't the resources to purchase a new, summer stock and his

Hong Kong distributor had flatly refused to extend him a line of credit for a supply of the goods.

"I had no right to travel to Amsterdam," the young man thought to himself.

The thing is that only a week ago, Samusis the younger had celebrated his birthday in the following manner: he flew to Amsterdam, popped into his favorite house of pleasure, spent some hour and a half in the company of smooth-skinned Celeste, and returned to New York the same night on the red-eye flight.

"Oh, how good it is to have money, youth, health, yard-wide shoulders, six feet in height, an intelligence that could boil water, and all the rest," thought Samusis the younger onboard the Boeing 747, pushing back his plush seat in the nonsmoking section. A meaningless smile flashed across his lips. So much water under the bridge! Well no, not in the sense of time; time here is beside the point—the difference is the way one feels about oneself.

Samusis the younger reached for the wallet in his pocket, took out of it a crumpled roach, turned his face towards the crosswalk, and lit up using a plastic Bic lighter and, sheltering the roach from the rain in his palm, took a deep toke. He sensed a pleasant iciness in his lungs.

"It seems that I am an incurable romantic after all," he thought to himself.

"Hey, pal. How much are your umbrellas?" the policeman's voice thundered above his ear. . . And so we will leave Samusis the younger in his, to put it mildly, complicated situation, the issue here being not so much the marijuana but his expired street vendor's license. Just read my lips: he went and got himself into some deep shit. Well, what can you do about it? He got himself into it, and he'll have to get himself out of it—he's not a child any longer.

Leaving Samusis the younger behind in the rain with a confused expression on his face, now turning red, let us for a change tell you about Zoya Samusis—there's no need to jump anywhere in our thoughts for this purpose as the rest of the story takes place in the present moment. Zoya, at her forty-six years of age, had managed to retain her former good looks, even though she had noticeably gained weight. Learning about her husband's demise, she reached his midtown workplace in a jiffy and, huffing heavily, ran into the office on the twenty second floor, saw her husband's corpse lying on the carpet with his purple-blue manhood peeking out of its fly and, sobbing loudly, hiked up her pinafore, shed her panties, and for the eyes of all to see, started humping our Henry Samusis. Somebody hissed: "She's lost her shame entirely!" She answered with some delay. Tears were streaming down her puffy cheeks and she wiped them off with the tie belonging to the departed, while not ceasing for a second to love her husband.

"Judge not lest you be judged," she finally proclaimed.

The wallet of the deceased suddenly reappeared all by itself.

Calming down, Zoya lay down beside Henry. They still made an attractive couple. What will she do without him? By education, she's a commercial artist. Hadn't worked in about twelve years. Try to find another man? But whom? However, it's much too soon for her to think about that. . . She raised herself up from the floor, straightened out her pinafore and approached the window. Outside, the workers were still busy maneuvering the letter "A".

"NAM," Zoya read what was left of the original two words.

"Mrs. Samusis," the head of the department called out to her.

Zoya looked back inside. In front of her stood a stout, grey-haired man wearing expensive, bottle green suit and a dark yellow tie speckled with white polka dots. His brown shoes with tassels were shined to a genuinely blinding sheen. His cufflinks—well, his cufflinks would require an entire story. Zoya had never seen such cufflinks before. You could see right away—these are expensive cufflinks. Just one such cufflink was easily worth three hundred dollars. The frames of his glasses, the tinted lenses—likewise expensive. The smell of his eau de cologne—expensive. Haircut, expensive.

"Mrs. Samusis, I ask you, Mrs. Samusis, to please accept my most sincere condolences. Believe me when I say that for all of us, for this entire department, the loss is irreplaceable. And only this year, I intended to personally propose his candidacy for a promotion. Moreover, I don't doubt for a second that the board of directors would have accepted my nomination. Mrs. Samusis, if there is anything I can ever do for your son—I know he's a budding businessman—a single word from you and I will do everything in my power. This death is a blow to the entire company. . . And now, with my apologies, would you please forgive me, but our workday lasts till five o'clock. Be so kind as to wait downstairs in the vestibule. They will soon come for the body; I have already made arrangements. Once again, forgive me, but. . . Business is business," he finished his extended outburst in a somewhat embarrassed tone.

Zoya Samusis was standing beside the window and, it seemed, had not heard a thing. Or she heard him but failed to understand anything. Or she understood but didn't think it required a reply. Or she wanted to answer but didn't know how. And only the blue vein on her left temple was thumping faster and faster. Without uttering a sound, with a single glance she took in the entire office, made a sharp 180 degree turn and without looking at anyone, briskly took off for the exit. And only at the very threshold did Zoya slow her pace and, directing herself to all at once, strained out through her teeth:

"Creeps, all of you aren't worth his little pinkie! If you only knew how he despised all of you! Without exception! Each and every one of you!"

She wanted to demonstratively slam shut the glass door, but she did not succeed in doing so—the door turned out to have been dampened. Cursing obscenely, Zoya rushed to the elevator, energetically pressed several times on the button labeled "Down," but the elevator, as though out of spite, had no intention of stopping for her. It was just then that Zoya experienced a full out attack of hysterics.

What else remains to be said? Time, of course, passed. How unfolded the fate of Samusis the younger, I cannot easily say. Did Zoya eventually remarry—I do not know. Samusis the elder was buried in a modest-sized cemetery in Forest Hills, not far from the little house where to this day live his aged parents. As for the joker from the HR department who had defiled the dying man in front of the whole department, in defense of the honor of the corporation to which Samusis the elder had given the best years of his life, I can report that the scoundrel was given a strong reprimand and his salary that year was raised only 2.5% instead of the 5% he had expected. A lesson to be learned; next time, he'll play it a little smarter.

*translated by Alex Cigale*

# Chronicle of a Murder

Second husband of my first cousin Marina Theodorovna, for-mer rationalizer Alesha had bad luck. And it was slowly be-ginning to dawn on him. Let's face it: an isolated episode of ill fate may be a coincidence, but what do you propose to do with a streak of bad luck the width of your youth and the length of the Avenue of Labor Veterans? Ignore it? "I'm a big schlimazl," la-mented my first cousin Marina Theodorovna's second husband, former rationalizer Alesha, but she still loved him very much and was very jealous (especially of other analysts). He got regular scratch treatment of his hirsute back, on Saturdays he got *grenki* (he liked them with honey), and at night he got almost anything he requested from his spouse in hot and timid whisperings di-rected squarely into her white nape.

Backseat rationalizers of Alesha's sort didn't exactly get the royal treatment at the institute for noxious gases. And so when one day he overreached himself and had some three years of particularly putrid air and passport restrictions, while a quick ride over yonder hill continued to tempt him with stylish and comfortable footwear and crackers to go with his aluminum-clad beer, it seemed like an appeal was out of the question. Who could resist the call of permanent residence, there! (beyond the sea. . .)—a temptation worthy of Dante's quill. But all of the be-hind remained above, in distant Novocherkassk, with winters so damn dreary and cold that even your average laborer in noxious gases was apt to wail with the bards (e. g. Okudzhava, Vizbor, etc.).

These days, seven years down the road in San Jose, after the untimely demise of my first cousin Marina Theodorovna (heart) and the advent of a younger woman (Internet), who stood (heels on) a full head above him, and whom (heels off) he pelted with kisses on midriff and clavicles, survivor of Marina Theodorovna, former rationalizer Alesha was butcher to Silicone Valley. No smirking, please: certainly not as glamorous as your new-fangled job, but quite enough to live on, even if you do have to get up early for it. Recall the carcasses of Soutine, especially of the green (rotting) period. So did former rationalizer Alesha, survivor of Marina Theodorovna, my first cousin, replacing oil on canvas with cleaver on marble, so to speak.

Then he and the woman (Valentina "push to shove" Ots) parted ways. Since then she's bagged half the town. The other half she'd bagged while they were still living together.

Whenever (quite often) former rationalizer Alesha confronted Valentina concerning matters of infidelity she at first denied everything, then cried and cursed a bit, then seeing that beau had a strong case broke down and confessed everything and—in a maneuver designed to soften the horn—graciously offered to do it the back way. That's how she liked it anyway, but during the act she screamed bloody murder, so that he'd know the sort of torture she was enduring for his sake. As a result she gradually trained Alesha to do it in the ass whenever she liked, as evidenced by a humorous letter sent out to a girlfriend in Minneapolis.

But this is not what the story is about. The story is about the time that Alesha moved out to New York and ran right into old Valentina Ots—this was at a party given by some Chelsea veteran, a quadriplegic hyperrealist, by the end of which, by way of slim promise of possible intimacy (Alesha had been going through a period of involuntary abstinence, which detail was writ large on his still relatively unspoiled face) she had ensnared Alesha in a plot to rob an Azeri multimillionaire that lived at the corner of Park Ave and 79th St., and the operation was more or less a success. Except that they hadn't worked out in advance what they'd do with the body. Because, how was anybody supposed to know that rich cock would actually be there himself and even put up a fight of sorts?

"What's gonna happen to the money?"

"What do you mean what? We split it, obviously."

"Halves?"

"Nah, I thought I get all, give you a receipt."

"Not funny."

"Yes, halves and haves, and have some more."

"And the body?"

"Maybe they'll take it at The Salvation Army?"

"Maybe you'll cut the moronic jokes? Just for the rest of the day, how about it?"

"We'll just drop it off at my folks—they don't do dick anyway, except watch the soaps all day."

"Valentina, please. I'm tired."

"Poor body. You used to get tired back then too, when you were slaving at your meat."

"Yes, I got tired then too. What about it?"

"And you didn't give it to me like I needed it."

"You got enough."

"I needed more."

"Enough."

"Out of curiosity, you didn't screw me because you didn't love me? Or because it didn't interest you?"

"How about when that rich cock was screwing you—what was that like? Were you getting enough then?"

"That's totally irrelevant. It was a means to an end."

"No, you answer the fuckin' question. What was that like?"

"That was like the fucker was johnny cum lately a minute into it. I didn't even feel it."

"Do I hear a note of disappointment?"

"No, you must really be fucked in the head. Are you seriously jealous of the corpse in the trunk?"

"Answer me. Were you disappointed?"

"I was indifferent. Impartial. I couldn't give a fuck. Calm yourself."

"Impartial blowjobs? An indifferent dick-in-your-mouth?"

"Shut up, idiot. Watch for the tunnel."

"You brought cocks home even back in San Jose. I was hacking up dead meat so we could pay the mortgage, and you were fucking them. Filth."

"You want to have this argument right now, Aleksei? You want to just push me right over the edge right here? Coming up, you fucking moron! There's diamonds in that glove box worth give or take a million. How long till you make that kind of money in your rotten meat shop? Maybe a couple of lifetimes! What could you do without me? I'm listening. What?"

"Then what the hell did you need me for? What, nobody else had a car? You got half of Queens in bed with you."

"I'll tell you what for, you prick. For pity. You got that? I pitied you. When I first let you—that was me pitying you. I even lived with you out of pity, because you're a loser. A pitiful loser."

"Pity? What happened to love? Ass fucking also a form of pity?"

"No, I'll die, people. Love? What language is that, you cocksucker?"

"That cocksucker will cost you."

"That's what you are, cocksucker."

"I'll pull over right here, and that's the end."

"Two cocks that's the end. I'll call the cops. Capiche?"

"And then what? One-way to Timbuktu? You're the one that hooked him, and booked him."

"Am I? Prove it! There's your prints all over the place in there. Your fingers did the walking. Hahaha!"

"Shut the fuck up. I swear I'll fuck you up next second. Take this hand and do it."

"Like the old times? San Jose? You beat me then, no?"

"Cause you ran in the bushes with whoever happens."

"Cause you were nothing. And you fucked like nothing. Hence the bushes. More fucking, less bushes. Got it? Limp dick."

"Cunt."

There is a bit more to the story—and that's the end part. Valentina shot Alesha there in the car, not far from Elizabeth, NJ. Details as follows: he raised his hand, as though intending to strike, just to scare her a bit—she drew a gun from her purse to stop him—he grasped the barrel of the gun with his left hand—she did not intend to pull the trigger (so she told the detective). There was a loud noise and the car swerved abruptly to the shoulder. Lots of cops showed up. Two ambulances. She was arrested and tried. She had shot him through his hairy chest. Both the back and the chest were hirsute. Had to shave it for the autopsy. Not a pleasant task. But then again butchery isn't for everyone either. Why didn't he try to find professional work here in the States? Why didn't he go for programming like the rest of them? Two reasons: language barrier; also he hated programming—wanted the road less traveled. And he got it: got mixed up with an old whore—she was already 34 when he found her—and lost his life. He maybe had 15 good years ahead of him. Productive, rationalizing years. Like a new and improved toaster. I'm just giving an example. Instead of 2 pieces it pops out, say, 10–15. That would work for large families, many kids. That's just the kind of fantastic imagination the guy had. He could have been a millionaire, living on Park Ave. Why did he have to get himself mixed up with her? She was already manifesting that whore gene back in Tallinn. I'm not lecturing, I'm just thinking out loud.

"Why did you leave me?"

"I left you?" (That's how it feels anyway, even if you're the one leaving. Feels like you're betrayed. Cheated. When you're cheated, you leave—she could have argued it that way instead of pulling a gun. But then she was going to get rid of him the good way or the bad way—the minx had already decided that back in the planning stages: she and the millionaire had had a thing going for like a year and a half, and if not for the tight fist she would have never taken it this far.)

"Maybe. But you, you never loved me." (Alesha would be useful, she figured along the way, or at the gallery, or even back in San Jose—she's like that—when shit goes wrong and somebody has to take the blame. She knew he wasn't too good about practical matters, and wouldn't have the money to get a decent lawyer, poor sob.)

"Like hell I didn't." (And he did love Valentina in his own way: what about the jealousy, the sex you know where, skins too. Smelled like shit afterwards, but who would know?)

"You didn't." (For christ's sake, just let it go. She's just trying to push you over the edge—and it's coming up.)

"You're gonna prove it?" (Good question. Is she going to prove it?)

"And you gonna prove that you did?" (Also a good question. There is much in love—and out of it—that simply must be taken on faith. How do you prove feelings? With words. And deeds.)

"I don't know," (he could have said. Sometimes deeds express little more than the deeds themselves. See explanation below.)

"Presents, yes?" (Yes, there you go. Maybe if he would have mentioned the presents—and he did stack them up back in San Jose—maybe she would have thought twice about dipping into her purse.)

"Yes." (And they weren't cheap either. See list below.)

"Vacations abroad, yes?" (Oh yes: in Amsterdam they got stoned to all devils, got to India a few times, puked in the canal—that was Venice.)

"Yes." (No, she couldn't possibly deny what was self-evident.)

"So what?" (That's Valentina once again, still pushing him on toward that edge. Nice girl. What else did she want then?)

"So nothing."

"So what?"

"What the hell else did you want?" (Lobsters by the sea, check? Puking in the canal, check? Check, sunset in the background. Oysters on a balcony in San Diego, check?)

"Fishing with the Kramarovichi, three checks? (The Kramarovichi were his friends, also from Novocherkassk, who had a pretty decent house in San Diego.) Flounder the size of the Sunday *Chronicle*, check? Gallery openings, check?" (Hold that one, not too many galleries in San Jose, and at the time of their meeting in New York he had been living with an old pal, looking for a place—everything had gotten horribly expensive, what with Brooklyn, and Queens, and Williamsburg, pass, pass, pass. Everything is much, much too expensive. Not exactly gallery mindset.)

Alesha hacked up the millionaire. Valentina's lawyer proved it was a crime of passion (Alesha's passion, that is) with Valentina as accomplice. She got ten years.

Here's what he got her: a lamp from Tiffany's. Gloves and a scarf—pricy, Dior maybe. Flat-screen TV on a stick: Surround sound. Armoire. Set of silver ice skates. With bells of some sort. Playing dice carved from the bones of rare animals (that was the butcher talking). Made bubkes, but still very generous. Kaput Alesha. The rationalizer went cunt up. Dead and buried.

*translated by Sergey Levchin*

# Five Easy Pieces

## I

*Presto con espressione*

The balding manikin with a sour, earth-toned expression (hereinafter: Fima Mekhanik, papa's partner and sidekick—for a time the two ran a shop out of a Chizhikov basement: papa's specialty was clockworks and knockoffs, Fima took care of the boys from the commerce squad—things were going swimmingly for a while, until papa got pinched, of course. Now this uncle Fima Mekhanik) once had the audacity in mama's presence—rest easy, mama—what a refined woman she was! loved Brahms to distraction! knew 29 different fish sauces! recited Pushkin in mass quantities—sister and I used to tease her and say she even knew the 10th (torched) chapter by heart—now this thrice-cursed Mekhanik once had the audacity in mama's presence to reflect unfavorably on the poetic talents of one Rozhdestvensky, mama's idol of sorts. The conversation turned—if memory serves me yet—on the universally and regionally beloved song "Wedding Feast." Filth (as we had dubbed Mekhanik) was especially incensed by the following lines:

> The squeeze-box roared
> and silence took its bow...

First he sang these lines in mock falsetto, rolling his eyes miserably and gesturing with his bulging larynx; then he proceeded to disparage the poet, imitating his speech defect—hitting below the belt, if you ask me—and finally, in the guise of an old world solicitor, he marched up and down our wretched kitchen, bobbing his head like a crazed canary, and implored the water heater (all the while darting suggestive glances in mama's direction) to please tell him whether the anthropomorphization of silence in the pastoral-realist genre perpetrated by this—god help him—child of the muses were not in fact—enough already, and will you not just shut your trap or do you need some help with that, you think everything is permitted as soon as papa goes under, reprobate!

Hearing the desperate cries emerging from the kitchen—mama apparently didn't let the visitor's lilac blazer and brass buttons keep her from enacting a swift preventative measure right where she stood and had dumped a bowl of summer borscht—greens, hard-boiled egg and sour-cream to taste—over Filth's pate—Lucy (sister) ran in from the living room holding together her denim robe: she had been practicing scales under the steady hand of nihilist-violinist Serezha Antonopoulo, star student at the conservatory and grandson of the great pediatrician Sergei Antonopoulo-Sergeev.

"Mama!" cried Lucy, "Mama, what is the matter with you!"

"Nothing, Lucia," mama said imperiously. "Lucky for him it was cold, bambina. Scum." She pretended to spit.

"Eva! What'd I do? What?" whined Mekhanik, carefully probing his ears for strands of limp dill.

"You know what," said mama, closing the discussion. "Filth."

## II

*Andante e cantabile*

I knew her by sight. She went around with upperclassmen. That's how they said it in those days: went around, going around. Full speed, too. She was especially popular with the second-year morons (an unwholesome gleam in their eyes)—made like she didn't mind their crude jokes and the stench. They were all smoking already. If you slipped the doorman at the hotel a few rubles he came back with a pack of America, tossing a quick glance across his shoulder. "America" was anything foreign-made; that included the Eastern Bloc. I watched her peach-colored dress dissolve into the warm light of the Palais Royal—her movements pierced my heart, and I would sink to the floor (figuratively, for the most part, but sometimes I dropped down on a bench to still my thoughts and the pounding in my chest). She moved like a real pro, a butterfly from flower to flower. She moved and her movements troubled the delicate retina with waves of varying frequency, though it was largely the red of traffic lights. She crossed the street and put out the lights all along the alleyway, so that you couldn't decide whether it would be best right now, or a little later, when the streetcar comes screeching around the corner. Horses were more or less gone by then—there was only one left: it had been reorganized into a children's attraction (5 kopeks apiece for a whiff of manure)—back to nature, keep the coachman kicking a while longer. Domestic "beetles" and "handicappies" displaced the last of noble beasts; her dad was missing a leg too, and his prosthesis creaked eloquently of the war—still a recent past—and the "earned" automobile, the bastards at the executive committee have been five years "working on it." A marvel of laconic rhetoric—the stump—could be glimpsed between the fraying cuff and brown boot.

She flung open the window to their (brother, wife from Simferopol) basement apartment, letting the fog creep in—creeping where I dared not dream to creep—and the Opera House moved closer somehow—they practiced arias in there all day long to the rumble of the perennial milk queue just outside. Father snoring on the couch in front of the "Ruby" tube, imminent heroic harvests (near) and workers' strikes (far) invading his dreams.

Sometimes she dragged her worn heels across the lining of your feverish brain—and you could close your eyes, but couldn't stop your ears, especially with your hands full, which often they were. Not necessarily clean, always cascading down to her ass her hair effused a thick, maddening scent. By April everything was flowing underfoot, and elsewhere. White stockings, tan knees around exam time, going up, all the way up under her skirt. I'm not going, though. I get to stay home, in the dark, I get to rub up against the mattress and curse into the pillow. Why—why is it the thing that you want most is the thing you can't have? Do you want it because you can't have it? Do they keep it from you so that you'd want it? Forbidden fruit... forbidden by whom? Show me the cocksucker that forbade it! Write it all over the fence, sure—but don't you look! Scratch it into every wall—but you'll never touch it!

I took cold showers... I tried to build up muscle desperately before summer—then I'd have something... I scrubbed my skin until it bled, I did push-ups anywhere I could drop down. Next-door Boris, an enthusiast of physical culture, chuckled and flexed his pecs in approbation, gave pointers.

Meanwhile occasional birds were already taking flight and sending back wondrous epistles from Vienna. "Beautiful! Unbelievable! You'll need some dough. Linens and optics do well." In another letter someone was pouring out praise for the Bruegel room at the Kunst-something-or-other.

She sat on the bench beneath the monument—she was being groped mercilessly. I watched them from behind a display stand, and I could see everything clearly: he was kissing the dewy nape of her neck. You bastard! I took my time pouring gasoline from a rusty can over his head, then I lit a match and touched it to the root of all evil: the root erupted in flames, hissed, bubbled—it had glands, as we recently learned in school—and then his body burned to a crisp and disintegrated. There was nothing left to bury except his College of Commerce insignia and the flame-retardant soles of his worn-out boots. His friends dressed as firemen attended the funeral under the sign of brass.

## III

*Vivace, ma non troppo*

Our fathers were friendly, mothers—tolerant. We couldn't stand each other, though. We could just stand each other, and that was about it. He was two years older. When you're fourteen that's a whole generation apart. Sunday mornings after *Hello There with Galina Novozhilova* papa (out on good behavior) took me in tow and together we'd go off to shoot the crap over at their place. He was never there, though: Kharitosha is taking the air with the young ladies. The table had already been set; papa produced a bottle of cold Stoli from his bag and Fima Mekhanik clapped his hands in mock surprise, mugging, squinting, zeroing in. The first went down with no chaser, the second was chased with a whiff of rye crust, and only after the third the magical combination of mackerel-sprats-herring-in-cream-boiled-potatoes-scallions-in-oil&vinegar made its ponderous appearance and was plundered barbarically for what seemed like an eternity punctuated by the smacking of lips, picking of teeth, dubious anecdotes, toasts to homecomings, to absent (briefly, but mercifully) spouses, and—Yulik, quick, make like you're deaf—to the ladies and to the whores.

Kharitosha is taking the air with the ladies. Those words pierced my heart. You were going around with girls—I wasn't. You could play the guitar—I couldn't. You had records—I had nothing. You wore corduroy bells and platforms... What the hell did I wear, I'm asking you? One time you said, "Don't fart if you can't shit," and you took the guitar out of my hands. That was when I messed up on "Lucy in the Sky." I had played the wrong chord—I didn't kill anybody, you know. You'd think it was the goddam Beethoven's *Ninth*. You were cruel and pitiless.

And I still wanted to be your friend. I wanted to go over to your house on holidays. I was never invited. I wanted so many things: your hair, your dandy monocle hung from a silk cord, your silver cigarette case with the mysterious engraving "Siege of Pleven." I watched you sweet-talking the girls, you were so cool, so confident. . . I wanted to play "Don't Let Me Down" just like you, tossing back my hair. . .

That summer I often ran into you in town—you always had a stack of records under your arm. "How's the old man," you'd ask, indifferent. "Thanks," I'd say, "he's doing better, should be out soon." He wasn't better, though, he was doing worse in fact—you knew that, of course—but it gave me intense pleasure to think that we were having a real conversation, almost as equals, and that other kids could see me talking to you and even asking you for a smoke.

"A smoke is better when you stroke, my young fellow," you retorted, but produced a cigarette nonetheless and extended it to me with an imperious hand. Fuck you.

"Not funny," I muttered and asked for a light, but you were already walking away, leaving me at the intersection (Greek and Lenin) with an unlit Opal.

"Gotta run, sorry chum," you winked and then called out, "It won't light if it can't stand upright. . ."

And I knew exactly where you were running to.

## IV

*Capriccio: Andantino grazioso*

Ostensibly things were more or less the same: oars, hands gripping the oars, rowers at their seats, life vests on rowers, their banter: gentlemen! one either rows forwards or one rows backwards! And yet there was something. . . What about the gang of stout, broad-bottomed lads in sailor suits—for some time now their shrill laughter has been perfectly audible to him, lying back in his chaise longue, half-dozing, still trying to wrest some speck of meaning from a curious leaflet she had left lying on top of her towel as if by accident. God knows what she meant by it. . . "Several Introductory Remarks on the Effective Methods of Breeding Artiodactyla in Captivity." Artiodactyla could be anything, but in captivity? A direct hit.

Her name seemed somehow old-fashioned, a remnant of the already fading '80s—L. She even wore a black velvet beret with the ribbons turned to one side; wouldn't go anywhere without it! But she could be persuaded on occasion to bury her neatly-groomed head in your chest or brush the tip of her tongue across your lips furtively, twisting her neck to spy on the bald conductor on the back platform. She also stuffed ticklers into her corset like an untouched schoolgirl, and clicked her tongue half-seriously when your dreaming hand crossed the line to caress her firm, pale expletive and a film of dew lined the nape of her neck and the underside of her alabaster ears.

Men with whom she had been intimate are likely to remember for some time the crackling of the fireplace on Marazlievskaia, eternal migraines, and a few blond ringlets belonging to a childhood friend, curled neatly into a tin marked "Fleurs d'Orange" and kept in a trunk by the cheval glass. He loved her cautiously, even fearfully—he didn't want to ruin her indiscreet jewels before their time—knowing full well that in the end they must pass on to another—the rightful addressee—and that he was no more than a courier boy, who had peeked into the package from imprudent curiosity. . .

What painter, what photographer, what holographer! could conjure through the mystery of his craft a faithful (or even nominal) rendering of the profound despair of this young gentleman, whose twisted spirit surged dangerously close to the ground. No, the j.-a.-d. ingreses, the nadars, the Austro-Hungarian art collective *Ziptrulibbe*'s of today are all no match for it. The scene holds no rewards for the optic nerve that craves non-verbal stimuli. We must have the delicate art of literature, the subtle play of word and metaphor.

Officers came over in civvies, civilians stayed past midnight, until the fireplace grew cold, my dear. Whatever thoughts came were all wretched, but he was somehow sure that they were not his, that they—chance, overheard thoughts—would soon depart, taking their busy leave. He even raged—though his rage was subdued, so unlike the frothing rage of youth, when it is yet to be decided whether the world's an ass that needs milking, or you're the unicorn, sans appropriately positioned maiden.

Officers amused themselves with solitaire and traded exquisite military witticisms. One droll tale involving a grand piano and a giggling child of fifteen dressed in salwars and a ball gown stung especially. She played the songs of Beranger—they were played in every decent home in those days—two or three of Chopin's études with both hands, then the lieutenant-widower Amethyst had her on all fours. Amethyst's wife Alicia had run off with a touring animal tamer by the name of Ivan Fallens; one fateful day, when I. Fallens' attention was momentarily and casually diverted by an aging contortionist Polina Antonopoulo, Alicia, who had been quietly leafing through the *Journal d'Odessa* in the wings, was mauled by the Bengal tiger Tig, who had perpetually a foul smell about him... A dreadful, improbable demise! The clowns wailed, rubbing tears into their painted chins, the sharp irony of the anecdote dissolved in prolix delivery, the phrase "had on all fours" acquired a revolting undertone.

Meanwhile civilians passed the time battling the four seasons: friend of family, ill-starred wholesaler Podolsky embodied autumn clumsily, rustled dead leaves, migrated south, drizzled on his companions... Those evenings had become unbearable, that indolence, that Chekhovian spleen, that had churned out so many dismal pages and metastasized in places that were difficult to pronounce. How could it happen in this town, of all places!

This too fueled his rage. And it was becoming all too evident: he had grown irritable, even spiteful; nearly given up shaving, threatened to dismiss the cook—everything seemed sour, burnt, insipid.

You have forgotten him, my dear, haven't you? He adored you, brought you L'Origan by Coty, eternal bon-bons, orchids from Lappenstok, quoted from Mallarmé on every unsuitable occasion, touched his lips to the delicate toes of your feet, put his expletive between your fragrant hillocks. He was fresh then, wasn't he my dear? And you have forgotten him, haven't you? Just say: I've forgotten him, I've forgotten him.

"I've forgotten him. I've forgotten him."

"I don't believe you, my dear."

<h1 style="text-align:center">V</h1>

*Finale: Allegro con spirito*

Papa had grown very queer before his death. He wandered about town with his pants off and flirted with exemplary citizens (pictured full size on street corners); he admonished the soda-dispensing machines for corrupting our historically uncarbonated way of life; he shouted at the traffic cop, "Madam, you are simply ravishing! That club! Those shoulder straps!" He spent countless hours before Pushkin's monument, assuming contemptuous poses and repeating over and over "Heathen! ever heard of the mother tongue? The mother tongue, you heathen, ever heard of it?" On Tiraspol Sq. he dropped a ruble in the blind man's cup and demanded no less than 40 kopeks change; rebuffed, he cursed the invalid, calling him a dirty Gobseck and ended by spitting into his cup. The blind man railed back with "That's what you are! And a thousand times that!" and tried to shove his knee into papa's crotch. But papa easily eluded him and ran to the other side of the square, waving over his head a great box of Turkish delight marked "Meteor" (product of Rosa Luxemburg Confections)...

In the hospital papa explained to us the precise meaning of the term "dissident," which Lucy and I had mistaken for a variety of antiperspirant.

"Nonsense!" cried papa in great disappointment. "A dissident protests, questions, sticks out in the notation...—like Lenin's wig. You have to understand one thing, children: dissent is possible in all weather conditions. All you have to do is run out in the pouring rain rather than cats and dogs and consider the act as occurring not, let us say, within a binary system, like some of those clowns do, but at certain points between, shall we say, two and number two—and you will see precisely what I mean without any great difficulty."

Papa always appreciated a sound philosophical discourse, but in confinement his appreciation had turned into a strange addiction. Had he been born into another time he would have seen great many admirers gather about him and bear him up in the air. As it happened papa was "borne up" only twice in his adult life: the first time by orderlies at the asylum, and the last by us—mama, myself, Lucy and Serezha Antonopoulo—en route to the Jewish cemetery.

"There comes a time in the life of any athlete," papa preached from the hospital bed, "when all the prizes and titles, roaring crowds, beautiful women—all of it recedes into the background. You go out there to do what you've always done, and you just hope nothing falls out of you while you do it. And if there's somebody that does it better—why there's always wider and deeper out there... You just have to love each other, children, and remember to love others, ok? That's what our starry papa said. And if you can't love each other, just pretend. Nothing can be easier."

Nothing, papa? What about hate? Really, old man! Hate is far easier! You're no better than a child, really. Are we just going to love anybody that gets in the way? What about your old Mekhan-ik, who sold you with all your innards—shall we love him too? What about Kharitosha, who frequently and with gusto expletive my one true love? And this fucked up expletive-ass life, with all its putrid corollaries and unwholesome swelling on the third day? Love that too, papa?

"Yes," said papa. "And quit cussing."

"That's right," said papa. "For how else?"

"Si," said papa. "Certamente."

"There," said papa. "Not as dumb as you look."

"Ah!" said papa. "Catching on, eh?"

Papa died with a mischievous—and slightly disdainful—ex-pression on his pallid face. Noting also the very tip of his tongue protruding from under his sparse mustache, one could speculate that his last movement in this world was to mock some undis-closed person, or perhaps to flirt halfheartedly with the nurse on duty. A less likely interpretation—though not entirely impossi-ble—is that he had intended to affix an imaginary stamp to some non-existent envelope, but in the end decided that it would get there just as it was.

*translated by Sergey Levchin*

# The '90s

These little knobs, and these, and those bigger ones, about yea-big, and then up above, next to a box under the fly, those enormous knobs, I've never seen any like them, are they all only my imagination, or are they actually there: are all these tiny, medium-size and humongous knobs some inseparable part of reality? In other words, do you see them? Huh? You don't? OK, let's move on.

In theory it's all very simple: a certain objective irony watches over us; here I am in Moscow, trading in pig iron and structural steel; I'm seeing a captivating Moscow University student, and right now she and I are, say, at the theater, and during intermission I indulge her at the snack bar, I'm trying to soften the girl up with eclairs. But that's in theory. In practice there is also a subjective irony, and both this ironic subjectivity and Aleksandra herself are in a constant state of flux. And that confuses me. It does.

The will to spectacle and illusion, unlike the will to knowledge and power, is merely another form of fundamental cynicism. This particular spectacle, as far as I can tell, Aleksandra doesn't care for much.

"Too much noise. And it's not funny," she confided briefly, then sat down again and didn't stand up until it was over.

She's so sweet. She drives me crazy. I haven't felt like this for a long time, really.

What is this? Is it my imagination, or that box over there, look, with knobs about the size of Jupiter, does Aleksandra like that box? Or is it the other way round, I should like that box? So many questions, questions at every turn! Why, I wonder, do the gods reside only in the inhuman, hide in it, in objects and beasts, in the realm of silence?... Let the human-god be absurd. A god who throws off the ironic mask of the inhuman, who abandons the bestial metaphor where, in silence, it embodied the principle of Evil—this god acquires a soul and a face, and so takes on all the hypocrisy of human psychology.

"The golden belt is loosed," thought Aleksandra, falling asleep, "the swaddling-clothes fall, and Apollo already demands his bow, his lyre, and proclaims his future prophecies for all to hear."

And meanwhile, or a little earlier, the stranger A. in the box paused, then intoned, "Oh, I'll kill you!"

At this point let us digress for a moment. It has more than once been noted that we are incapable of perceiving the mental Other in the same way that we perceive the physical Other. All we can perceive is some synthesis of the psychic, attainable by enumerating a series of external signs of a psychic state, well I don't know, say a jaw twitching and/or large beads of sweat forming on the forehead and/or angry whispers, which, having compared them to the neutral voice of the television commentator, say, or with the warm dry forehead of Aleksandra, we can define as signs of extreme agitation. The difficulty of the scene above lay largely in the fact that the stranger was located in a box and seemed impossible to observe. Moreover, his threat was uttered in a very even voice and aimed at no one in particular. It was possible that he wasn't alone in the box, possible that he was thinking aloud or/and...

When I speak of the object and its fatal strategies, I am speaking of a person and of his or her inhuman strategies—I didn't say this, somebody nearby did. A little later he explained.

"I've carried out your assignment," came the words from the stage. "Yesterday at the theater I announced that you'd come down with brain fever and that probably you were already dead and gone."

But that's a quote.

And that's a quote.

I've heard that somewhere before.

It was a quote.

Chatter is usually associated with the comic element. This element includes, for example, the idle chatter encountered in folklore, where it, in conjunction with the fantastic, and absurd or confused speech, serves to express buffoonery, or chicanery which lulls the intellect to sleep. It should be noted that this tactic had brought about quite tangible results: Aleksandra was asleep on my shoulder, her mouth slightly open, her upper lip—nature, her lower lip—fate. I, obedient to that most ancient of instincts, was about to try looking through the corner of my eye into Aleksandra's mouth, but at that point the lights went down again and the third act began.

Two characters beside a small pond: a Red Army soldier with no arms and a White Guard soldier with no legs, perpendicular to one another. One of them was wearing a circle about two units in diameter, the other had no circle, but he thought he did, and this illusion made him vulnerable, although the White soldier didn't notice this because he was wracked by a cough. It was obvious that he was near death, to which the unhealthy flush that covered him from head to stump testified. On the far shore of the pond frogs were croaking, wheat was rustling, the sun was going down. The conversation was unhurried.

The first said: "This is mine, this is mine and this is mine, but that one, that'un and the one yonder—not, not, not. These here, these're mine, and these, but those—those aren't, not those either."

The second one asks: "Well whose are they?"

First: "Which, those?"

Second: "Those and those and those."

First: "Those are mine, these are mine, but these and those there—they're mine too."

Second: "But whose are those?"

First: "Those aren't mine."

Second: "Whose then?"

First: "Not anybody's."

Second: "That means they're not yours and not anybody's. So whose are they?"

First: "Not anybody's, I already said."

Second: "Then who do they belong to?"

First: "Nobody, I guess."

Second: "And the one's that are yours, they're yours by what right?"

First: "Well, in the first place I bought them, in the second I inherited them, in the third seized, in the fourth, penetrated, in the fifth, thought them through to the end, in the sixth, I like them very much, I quote them, I wear them around and never take them off or part with them, I repeat them to myself. But the ones that aren't mine I take off at night, I don't wear them, I forget, and I don't understand them at all."

Second: "Now about the ones that aren't anybody's. They're not yours and not mine. That means they're his, hers or theirs, right?"

First: "Right."

Suddenly there was a rumble, everything instantly went dark, and paradoxically only the vision of A., the stranger inside the box, was unaffected. This appropriated the emptiness, made it virtually palpable. Maybe you even wanted to think about something, but there were no things anymore. The young man without legs was embracing the young man without arms, they were laughing gaily, their conversation was free and easy, things no longer hindered them.

I sat there in my seat, afraid to move. I didn't want to wake Aleksandra.

For some reason I suddenly felt happy. It even seemed as if somewhere under my heart, a new person was beginning. That new person was me, but smaller, and a little freer, gentler, kinder than me. Better, too.

Many things became clear to me that evening. For example, that the subject-object opposition is indeed unassailable and permanent, and one oughtn't cherish any illusions on that subject. And also, that first one should change the external, then become part of that external and only later, having acknowledged oneself a part of the external, transcend one's own self. But moving to another place, learning another language, or screwing another national—that's, begging your pardon, self-deception, that's just a change of set. It's like the "a year passes" program note between the second and third acts. A year doesn't pass between acts, it passes within them.

A shot came from inside the box, then the sound of a body falling from a chair, then muted music, and after that, sparse applause.

And you know those knobs that it all started with really were only in my imagination. I say "only" not in any pejorative sense, but with one wish: to emphasize that they stayed practically within the borders of my imagination.

And meanwhile or maybe a little earlier, out on the Old Arbat, up towards Smolenskaya Square, Alyosha the seismologist was getting worked up over the following thought: I don't think I've got the strength of mind to move to Canada. In the first place, he was stewing, what will I do in a new country with no language, no money, no know-how, eh? In the second place, even if everything here is shaky and unstable and the best installations are totally inaccessible to the homegrown audience and my postmodernist friends are entrenched in NewYorkParisMilan and theaters are deserted and there are discos in the movie theaters and my wife's sick of it and I'm sick of her, still, begging your pardon, Nietzsche is coming out? Have I just put in the subscription to Schopenhauer the bard of pessimism or haven't I? Have they finally published Heidegger or haven't they? And damn, Moscow's beautiful after a rain, when the asphalt reflects all the children, the aging female intellectuals toting flags, the young people strolling in pairs and alone, the Airedale terriers—in a word, all the components of reality given us in sensations.

"To the State Duma Elections!! Vote for 'Russia's Choice'!!!" Alyosha suddenly cried out in a kind of funereal ecstasy.

A crowd of onlookers surrounded him and beat him half to death.

At the hospital an angel of the Lord came down and whispered these words in his ear:

"Getting burned by life is not the whole truth, Alyoshenka. Getting burned by life is just a kind of breather. You turn left, no thru way, it's blocked, got to detour; we circle round for ten minutes or so, find the house, but it's in the middle of a mudhole, no way in hell, and it's too late to go back, after one in the morning by now, and besides the whole place is stripped, the wallpaper's peeling. The burn heals, the memory stays, and for lack of any other news, that's all we have to work with. So think it over."

Alyosha died in his sleep of a brain hemorrhage. It happened in the year 2021 in Montreal. His wife never knew. She'd remarried, this time happily.

Meanwhile, at this very moment or a little earlier, a woman in New York was hiccuping, loudly. You remember sex, right? Her legs, and your kisses covering them? The desire surging beyond all bounds? The succulence? It was no accident Yelena Markovna laid hands on herself. In protest. She was unstable in both the financial and the emotional sense. Remember her tongue in your mouth at dawn? You forgot already. But I remember. Astor Place, by the cube. Garbage everywhere, and pigeons.

When the police arrived it was still early. She died in a foreign place, in emigration. Far from her home port. While back in her home port amidst lapping reflections somebody was rotting away, and everybody and their brother was peeing on him. Sweet young things squatted and peed, arms wrapped around fat knees. Their rumps gleamed white over the sleepy waters. Leskov, the commercial director of a small firm, peed too, jiggling his flabby little penis. And she left all this for some 'abroad'? What did she forget in that America of hers? Who was she there? A secretary. Period. But in her home port she could have pulled down her drawers just like everybody else, squatted, and pissed to her heart's content on the head of a certain disintegrating fellow named Rutabagov. I expect an intelligible answer here. Intelligible.

And her hiccups were a result of what, I ask you? Fear, a consequence of fear. Was a failed romance with a co-worker, the manager of one of the ten leading insurance companies in the greater New York area, really the sole cause of death in the case of Yelena Markovna Mironova, former artist from Yalta? And what's this crap about Yalta? She was never there in her life.

Remember your little vacation romance, the standard "last belch of youth"? You don't? And the warmth spreading all over your undershorts, you don't recall that either? Or how in New York it sparked again, your almost completely cooled... It's true, it's all true. And as a result she had the hiccups.

"So don't swallow, silly goose," you whispered affectionately, toying with her rubber friend.

"Good for the complexion."

And now she's gone. You're here, I'm here, her mother the linguist Averbakh is here, but Yelena Markovna's fucking done for. Artist, my ass! She should have stayed home in Yalta and kept her yap shut.

But you know her cousin Andrei Sevastianovich Avenger, who lived catty-corner from the Central Market, had a favorite little saying: "Plank-plankity-plank." Depending on the circumstances—which were always changing—he might use it to express either ... / or ... Once some little snotnose twerps began harassing him at a stand near the Baumanskaya metro station. He was stunned. Snotnoses! Who do they think they're threatening? They dare lay a hand on Avenger? Avenger! Aven... hey, gramps, stop hitting! That hurts! It was a joke! Plankityplank! Plankem! In the chops! Chops! I'll show you a joke! No respect these days. Alright then.

And uh, and uh, and up the hill came Katya. Pretty Katya breasts aheave, pretty Katya please don't leave. Plankity.

And now some truly unbelievable events were supposed to take place, with A. S. Avenger, pensioner, master-of-chess candidate, master craftsman, as their witness. Chessboard, chess pieces, cough, newspaper, engraved watch. She, Katya (or he, Katya, since Katya is actually a boy named Trofimov, but that was to be explained later on) was supposed to become an unsuspecting witness to the death of Avenger who like his idol Roland Barthes but about fourteen years later would get hit by a truck. And at the height of summer too! The hired killers frolic. We hear bursts of laughter. Yeah, laugh away! Katya twangs her guitar. And now here's the song performed by the boy Trofimov in his rather pleasant voice.

> Well, people can wash out their linen
> And time it can heal all our hurts
> And mama's gaze, secret, secluded,
> Is balm to my poor aching heart;
> To end it all, leap off, and hope that
> You splatter yourself into matter and stuff,
> But you catch on an edge
> And you bounce off the ledge,
> And you fall hard, but not hard enough.
> Oh mama's secluded, still glances
> They heal all my poor broken bones,
> And so do my mama's soft panties
> And so do my mama's silk hose.

And at that very moment, and not a minute sooner, a very small boy woke up in his crib and saw a bird outside his window, eating flesh. Feeding on human flesh.

"Now here's something new," thought the boy.

"I'm a failure, it's obvious," thought the small boy's father, a young, not very self-assured nuclear physicist.

"Don't be silly. . . " said the small boy's mama, snapping her pantyhose at him; she was a nice-looking woman, a psychologist, I think.

They'd met at a disco. She was dancing a slow dance. Her eyes were like two emeralds. The small boy's father sensed right then that he could be happy with her anywhere, even in New Zealand.

The older kids in the building were picking on the boy. They'd been threatening to rip his throat out, but somehow had never got around to it. But now. . .

Hop-bilibilibili-hop, woman of my dreams. At this point the boy's father intervened. The older kids scattered, the boy was in tears.

"Are you a man or not? Stop blubbing like some girl then."

New Zealand: never been there, but I'll try and describe it anyway. Here we go—McDonald's, gas stations, movie theaters, outdoor concerts, incredible sunsets.

Of course it would be nice to tie all this in with national and even global trends in ecology, or developments in Africa and the Crimea. But everything is already interconnected. If you don't believe me, ask Leibniz. So let's just cut the complaints, alright?

Anyway the boy's name was Polikarpov. He eventually became a famous cellist. His father received a Nobel Prize, his mother too.

*translated by Jane Miller*

# Love Gone South

Babushka with no teeth didn't look so hot. That figures. She had stood the shafts of time, the jeers of grandchildren (dull, unkind amerikantsy). She dreamt of her native land (in this case Simferopol)—that's where she had been young, where first she felt sweet longing in her underbelly. . . there were teeth in that life, too: a dazzling row of ivories. What did she have here? Husband gone, spark out, children don't visit. They say it's too far. They're too busy. Busy with what? What are they doing, anyway? Maybe she was too busy to drag herself over there for six years, babysitting duty. Sweets and meats from Kolobok, regular delivery. Collaborators, she called them under her breath; and cried. Thank god for Anna and her husband—cultured and thoroughly decent people, and well-off, too (the rug from Cancun must have been over a grand); without them Babushka would be utterly lost.

Well, thought Babushka sans teeth, here comes old age. But it had already come. NTV was running an old Yugoslav comedy with a popular crooner from back in the day. But she didn't think it was funny anymore. And the thought of getting her teeth came only rarely these days.

She liked him right away. Nikolai wasn't very old—sixty-five is prime renaissance for a man. He also had a respectable business: a video rental store that he'd named See for Yourself. And he's been here forever, way before that lunatic lunged at Reagan to wow indifferent actress Farrah Falset. Nikolai's children are also in business—they have their own travel agency and a condo in Manhattan. He was bringing her flowers from day one, courted her gallantly, and gave her a dress that was as light as down, but also very warm, with a lining. One time he took her to a show—Hanging Left, a techno outfit from Zhitomir was in town. Then out to dinner. She didn't get that sort of music, confessed Babushka. She'd knocked back a brandy and sighed a bit first. It was just a lot of noise, if you asked her. Sofia Rotaru, that's more her thing. Nikolai said he didn't really get the music either—or music in general—but that you had to do something with yourself on weekends. That's when she showed him her shy, toothless smile—but it still came out very sweet and sincere. Because when you love somebody—when you want to be loved by that somebody—you may choose to overlook a good deal. And he overlooked.

Babushka's son Fimka, nicknamed Polygam, was a real-life fuck-up. How does a decent woman like that end up with a fuck-up—why don't you answer me? Take your time, think about it, then answer me. Accuracy is more important than speed, at least in this instance. He was going for a massage certificate, but that was too much for him, so he decided to go into business. His wife was head stripper. To what shall I compare her bust, the way it was back in that far off day? I don't know to what, honestly. Her first husband was a convicted felon—they barely let him into the country; he had to part with serious money to get in. Back then they generally kept convicts out with rare exception. She got pumped up with silicon when she was still a kid—obviously they'll take you more seriously when there's a lot and jiggly. . .

Fimka Polygam said to Elka: listen up here. You're a hot babe. I get a standing ovation for you in my pants, but you promise me scout's honor that you leave this dump once we get hitched. This is no kind of life for a hot awesome babe such as you are. You're so hot and awesome I'm dying, literally. Totally hot. Like Julia Roberts, but hotter. "Who's gonna take care of me?" said Elka, straight up. Fimka whistled expressively: "Hey!" and tilted his head to one side. So she showed him the Tower of Pisa with a view downtown, by way of appetizer. For those not in the know that's a kind of leaning hand-stand that defies description. Suffice it to say that Polygam whistled once more, this time even louder, noting that hot babe was also hot where it counts. "As above so below." The ancients said so, albeit under other circumstances.

Trouble is she was bunking with club management about that time—an old goumba Vincenzo Scarlatini, if memory serves me. This was a flabby jaundiced prick, but if licked on all sides it got hard and did its duty. He took her on when she was a young girl—did it as a favor to her husband. They were partners in a real estate scam back then. Felon hubby poured 3 mil into a Florida swamp one laundry day. The operation was running smoothly, but then the Italian caught sight of Elka in shades and a pink suit (this was at Pelmeni A Go-Go) and had a hormonal reaction between his legs. He poked around a bit in hubby's back ventures and then offered him a choice: either Elka changes sides, or you'll be digging yourself out of a real swamp for the next ten years or so. Took him by the balls, that is. Thus Elka transitioned from one set of hands to another. Since then she'd been pretty down on guys in general. What sort of business is that—she complained—am I a passing trophy with an ass? Certainly not. She was a handsome young woman, a skilled worker in adult entertainment. Yes... adults, mind you—that didn't include octogenarians with blue jelly where their legs should be. She could die from shame, strolling around seaside hand in hand. People were looking. That's how Elka ended up with Fimka.

Babushka liked her right away. Elka was a fine girl, kept house properly and threw together a sushi salad occasionally. Fimka's first wife was a Romanian national with a fake nutritionist's license—this was far better. There had also been a dozen or so short-order waitresses from Neptune that pranced about in slips all winter long (dears in headlights, she called them). Pneumonia was powerless. So was police. But this is not about them, anyway.

Basically the situation was unfolding no worse than the chair Babushka brought with her to the boardwalk on summer afternoons: it was precarious but lightweight, and had only to be set up in the shade, away from the noisy crowds. Doesn't seem so hard, does it? But go and find that shade, if you can. There isn't any.

Fimka, Elka and their brood had Seder with mother and there first made the acquaintance of a seemingly well-off gentleman in a collarless shirt from Versace with gold buttons. After the second cup it was revealed what the gentleman does "for a living" and Fimka Polygam saw with great clarity what the chance meeting could spell for his future. A business opportunity! This partner had to be apprehended right away, no later than the third cup, while he was still soft. It so happened that Fimka had this fantasy of selling a couple of films (adult content) starring none other than Elka. These were made by some NYU art-weirdos way back when she was just starting out in show business. In Fimka's great scheme of things they were to become a kind of launching pad for his career as producer, which was his great dream in life. Sweet ambition! But can a man not dream, especially if he is still under forty and living in the USA?

Nikolai was cautious though, and he cooled Fimka's enthusiasm, telling him curtly that he wasn't looking for new distributors. Not his typical ware, either. "But. . ." Nikolai held a long, meaningful pause, "considering. . ." and he held another pause, in the course of which Babushka went from crimson to deep purple—something she'd been doing a lot lately—"I could take a look," he concluded and glanced over at Elka, who was poking vaguely at a piece of gefilte fish.

They set the date secretly for next weekend chez Babushka. As it happened, Fimka's VCR was acting up.

They picked the time when Babushka paid her usual visit to Anna and her husband. That would be a good time, they figured. But... homo proponit, sed Deus has a habit of fucking with other people's business. It happened that Babushka got bored with her company: it was the same old conversation, same gossip, same memories. Sokurov's *Ark*! Tovstonogov's *Idiot*! Cancun in merry month of May! Alesha Shoikhet's daughter's wedding at the Kazanova. Babushka decided to take her leave· she'd never seen the *Ark* or Cancun, and had only a vague idea who were Shoikhet and Tovstonogov. If she wanted to sit and stare the whole time she could go home and watch her NTV. At least that didn't make her feel like an old fool.

Babushka came home earlier than usual. She slipped softly into the dark hallway and stood there, catching her breath and prying off her tennis shoes. Then she heard voices. And moans. Nikolai and Fimka were sprawled out on the couch, drinking American poison and exchanging monosyllables. Babushka looked over at the TV screen. She saw her dear daughter-in-law, still a child, really—saw her mons à la Khruschev—saw two muscular men having Elka in latest positions, first on the fridge, then by the sink, and then, by way of grand finale (oh, wicked shame!), using her face as a sort of human outhouse. Nikolai's voice—his casual remarks—reached her as though through a thick coverlet. Among other things he proposed a few additional episodes, sequels, as it were—Babushka lost consciousness. She fell to the floor, still in the hallway, hitting the side of her head on a bookshelf with the complete works of Ludmila Kupriyanova, an author of women's detective novels.

When Babushka sans teeth came to Nikolai was standing over her with a glass of seltzer, explaining as best he could that it was a business transaction, and a favor to Fimka, really. Fimka was also at her side, nodding vigorously and lecturing on trends in contemporary cinema and on marketability—this was America, he said, and the main thing is to get in the door, doesn't matter what your product is, as long as somebody's buying it. But Babushka refused to hear it; she just lay there, shaking her gray head. After a while she got up, still holding her head with one hand, smoothed her dress (Nikolai's gift) and showed Fimka the door in precise terms (scum, pervert). Then she asked Nikolai to leave also, though it wasn't exactly easy for her. He called her a dozen times afterwards, asking her to come see Eifman and Zemfira at the Millenium. What Eifman? What Zemfira?

At the end of her life Babushka was left with nothing. The promise of personal happiness proved short-lived. Now she sits all alone on her fold-out chair in the middle of the boardwalk; nothing gets through to her and nothing comes out, except her incessant muttering: "Whore. Whore. Goddam whore. Slut of a whore."

Fimka Polygam, her child, will soon make something of himself, wait and see. He'll probably become a producer. His kids from Elka, and the Romanian, will grow up and go to Harvard and Bard, like all decent children. But Babushka... how will she ever get over the shock?

That's the whole story. Last year Nikolai bought another video store. He also hosts a local radio show called *Ars Amatoria*. Fimka got his producership after all. His sex-musical *The Cherry Orchard* will be showing on cable come September. He and Elka split up. She married Jean-Claude Drissert, the one that made Proust's *Sodom and Gomorrah*.

Babushka... Babushka's case isn't so simple. Babushka is seriously thinking of going back to Simferopol. She's planning to have her teeth put in there. Somebody told her that the dentists there are decent, and they don't bite as much. Naturally, it won't be easy at first, digesting forgotten foods, communing with the half-dead. But it's not any better here, that's for sure.

My next story will be about Babushka—about her journey home. And about the healing power of native soil, especially after a long life abroad. No matter how you slice it: there's no place like it. No place like home that is. Some people had better think twice before leaving it.

*translated by Sergey Levchin*

# Rehearsal

"The writer Lev Nikolaevich Kafka was a total idiot." Let's say that, with this sentence, a certain someone or other wishes to express their relationship to reality, which does not exist. Then how may the statement—"reality which does not exist"—be understood? This, first and foremost, is reality which does exist, but that must be taken under the "minus" sign. Let me give you a practical example. You are riding the escalator, in the subway station, at Alexandrovsky Garden, in the direction signed "plus" while coming towards you are: a woman-pulmonologist, students at MGU, and a group of young businessmen lugging a suitcase-full of women's hose, and all of them are moving in the direction under the sign of "minus." In other words, they are part of that set I had earlier referred to as "reality under the 'minus' sign."

Now, why is it written above that "a certain someone" wishes to express, with the sentence "Lev Nikolaevich Kafka was a total idiot," their relationship to reality taken under the "minus" sign and then, if such a statement were justified, what is that relationship, and is it ever even possible for any sentence to express this relationship? However, before such questions may be answered, I would like to offer you the following concise composition I've titled "In a Puddle."

"Handicapped considered him a madman, and madmen a handicapped. But in reality, he was neither. He was lying at the intersection of two serpentine streets, being sniffed over by a homeless yard dog, and he was crying. The sky was being reflected in his eyes, in his tears, and in the puddle which, were he himself able to give us his own full account of the events, he'd be able to take credit for being the author of. How did he fall so low? Well, you just listen to me...

In 1989, he got jolted in the groin, and in 1990 he got three fingers of his right hand sliced off, the blood gushed onto his jacket and new pants but, goodness gracious, forget about the clothes... Ever since then, his reason had become muddled.

"Pop, come quickly! Mom's already naked!"—his son, little Grisha, would yell out the window, waving his puny arm at him.

And once, when he was riding the tram, some beggar who really stunk would not leave him alone and, the spittle flying, started reciting "The Sorrows of Young Werther" at him in passable German. Leosha, for that was the name of our hero, all of a sudden went amok. With a jerky movement of his right hand he poked out the beggar's eyes, both of them, with his pinky and with his thumb. The beggar bellowed like a beluga, laid a dump in his pants, and crumpled onto the floor of the tram car.

Leosha was released from prison, now much emaciated, in May of 1993. His cheeks had fallen in and his temples had turned completely grey. He had written to his son and wife daily, though it wasn't easy—to hold the stump of a pencil with two fingers, the thumb and the pinky. Meanwhile, Leosha's wife had time to unite her future with that of her renter from the provinces, whose business was in retailing cash and carry goods: beer, rubber genitalia, office equipment. Leosha, taking it personally, poked out the eyes of this rival also and, when he did that, the man roared like a bear. You might recall the beggar on the tram bellowed like a beluga, but the renter from Saratov, rolling around the parquet floor in a puddle of his own blood roared like a bear.

Leosha's wife, Lyudochka, bellowed like a beluga when Leosha, in the heat of passion, ill-treated her, kicking her in the face and on her breasts and in her stomach (she was in the fourth month of pregnancy). The neighbors howled like polar bears from the other side of the wall; Grisha, Leosha's son, yelled: "Don't hit

Mama, Papa! Mama's good!"—bellowing like a beluga. The boy would soon be turning fourteen.

And that is how Leosha came to lie at the intersection of two streets. "Good God, how much suffering there is in the world, how much malice, cruelty, deceit, and so little gentleness, tenderness, and love"—he thought to himself. "And these smells, these screams, these unbearable people. . ." But ain't that the truth, they are unbearable, they're even worse than Leosha. Leosha is just a schlub, the victim of a period of transition, but many are simply irredeemable scoundrels."

And now, let us turn again to the problem of reality under the "minus" sign. We'll begin with the fact that the writer Lev Nikolaevich Kafka does not exist in nature, nor did he ever exist. Of course, I could, this very second, take L. N. Kafka as my pseudonym, and if by writer we are to understand a person who makes signs on paper that then may be interpreted in one way or another by someone, then I, this very second, become the writer L. N. Kafka, according to our definition, a total idiot, something that still requires proof, except that I refuse to take for myself a pseudonym of any kind, so therefore the writer L. N. Kafka will remain an imaginary person, and as such, he may also be added to that set which comprises reality under the "minus" sign, not for the reason that he's moving toward us, but because he simply and entirely doesn't exist.

It is commonly known that such writers, the Count Lev Nikolaevich Tolstoy—one of the heroes of the journals of Sonya Behrs, and Franz Kafka—one of the heroes of the journals of the writer Franz Kafka, existed, but the writer Lev Nikolaevich Kafka did not exist until the first sentence of this text; and now, this writer exists as part of the set comprising reality under the "minus" sign, to which this text belongs, along with the someone or other composing this text. We may with certainty (and we note this in parentheses) assert that Kafka knew of Tolstoy and read Tolstoy, and equally, that Tolstoy could not have known about Kafka and read Kafka, just as the someone or other writing these lines read the one (Tolstoy) and the other (Kafka), but it would have been better if he had read neither, better had he read neither, better had he read neither, better had he read neither, better had he read neither, better had he read neither, better had he read neither, better had he read neither of them, at all. And why is that? Better for whom? This is the subject of another conversation, but for now, I'll just say that Lev Nikolaevich Kafka, in reality under the "minus" sign, according to the assertion of a certain "someone or other," was a total idiot, and that this assertion is justified, if even only because it has yet to be refuted by anyone.

And finally: Franz Kafka, Lev Tolstoy, and the author of these lines, "someone or other," do not simultaneously belong to any of the sets considered above, but we will need to address this issue in our next rehearsal and, for now, — just one more narrative, "On the Pier," whose hero (by the way, also a Leosha, Leonid Grigorievich) for the entire duration of the story stands still on a pier, which by the way is in a state of near-catastrophic disrepair, with the following thoughts running through his head. And so, without further adieu, "On the Pier."

"For some time he listened in silence, attempting to make heads or tails of this sensation, unlike any other he had ever felt, mentally clicking together his fingers, uselessly hoping to find the right words. But for whom? The right, the necessary words, pathetic for their imprecision and, to put it concisely, that are always a little off in hitting their mark. Maybe we can say this: he distinctly sensed how his present flowed into his past, so that the gulf Leonid Grigorievich sensed between them in an almost physical way narrowed and, being grafted together, was spanned by a thin but resilient layer of film. Am I speaking clearly now?

If the past may, conditionally, be imagined as a woman—you are running away from it, running away, and then it is running away from you, and then it up and freezes in the middle of the street leading toward the ocean and, turning toward you, with the forever pressing and rubbing sandals on its heels, sticks out its tongue at you and makes a funny, contorted face. . . and the present be imagined as a man, always and ever trying to reinforce its confidence in itself, and the bald spots are irrelevant here, the bald spots are a temporary phenomenon, it's not yet complete baldness after all, you can't argue against complete baldness, and the shortness of breath at thirty-something is also immaterial—then all this, if you will, is the coupling of the present and the past on the cooling sands of a deserted beach at night, with the medical scales standing in the wings, the past having had stubbornly resisted the whole time, but the present was persuasively persistent—making goo goo eyes and pretentiously quoting something or other out of Dante—and so their conjunction was, finally, consecrated.

You know what it is like at the end of May. Still cold, but already warm; you understand. There is a certain je ne sais quoi in the air, and Leonid Grigorievich himself is visibly changed, on the inside: his stomach lining abraded, the lungs worn out, the guts—turned to shit. 'Better look after yourself, or you won't be able to find a wife,' his mother had performed this leitmotif for him at every opportunity and upon every occasion: using the example of his friends, the example of people unfamiliar to him, without any precedent, with the look of her eyes alone, in reproach, but also without any etc. And he would just make light of it. Responded with a joke for a year, then a second year, five years he made light of it, and then he went and bought himself a decent suit, spent an entire month's salary on it and didn't even bat an eye, but clenched his teeth and bit the bullet, didn't even blink once. And so, in this suit, he was standing on the pier looking off into the distance, his hair getting tangled in the wind, the whipping coat-tails of his jacket giving him the appearance of a bird wearing a tie or, more precisely, a resemblance to an immature sea lion tossed by the winds of fate onto our southern shores. He was standing and, and I repeat myself here, felt as though his past and his presence were converging, and this sensation felt like a comfort to his soul. This is how he imagined the rest of his life to himself (he expected to live to fifty one): children (three of them), a wife (twenty three years old, raven-haired, a non-smoker), happiness (it is, essentially, different for each of us, but in just a couple of words: do not believe those who insist that it doesn't exist; it's untrue—happiness exists, and I had experienced it for myself some twelve years ago, during a basketball game, but I don't want to go on and on about myself, that's boring), interesting, well-paid work as a bourgeois writer producing cultural goods readymade for the market, which means recognition from a reading public and so at least some sort of status, well, and an accidental death in a drunken brawl, but that's still to come, at the very end. The wife places flowers on his grave, the children blink trying to understand where their papa's gone, and he, lying in the ground, and thinking to himself: 'Good Lord! Finally.'"

In the most general case, and this is such a one, I assure you, the following may be stated: time passes, places change, and the pain of loss transforms also, and we factor out here the word "passes" and isolate it outside the parentheses so that the result is: what passes is—time, place, the pain of loss—and it is precisely time minus place that the loss perceived as pain consists in; substituting "time minus place" for "pain of loss" our answer is: everything passes (time, place, pain of loss); distributing "passes" from within the parentheses we get: time passes plus time passes that is, twice as much time passes. In toto: from where I stand, I am looking into the distance. There, in the distance, in the future that is quickly approaching, stands Leonid, who likewise stands looking off into the distance, thinking: how quickly, after all, time passes, and also: perhaps this is so precisely because the past has started to blend in with the present, the real? Somehow we have to find the time, and in the past, there, there was always more of it. And also: that's all folks—knock-knock-knock, knock on wood—not too bad so far, God willing, hopefully, what's to come won't be much worse. And then he raps the knuckles of his fist three times on the wooden handrail of the pier, and he hears how, somewhere out in the fog a boat produces a sad-sounding "oo-oo," and he becomes melancholy, but not so much as for us to feel that we have to get it all down on paper, but just a little bit, just a touch so.

"May, and it's still cold," thinks our hero, to whom we, you will agree, have already become somewhat accustomed, and then he makes a cold 'b-r-r-' sound and vanishes into thin air and out of our field of vision.

*translated by Alex Cigale*

# The Last Words

Laid over mercilessly, alone on a half-forgotten freight, Joe "Tough Nut" Fink rolled into town—the same old town, where, according to Diana "Feeling It, Sweetheart" Noyse, he had spent his childhood dicking the birdies in the pear tree. They had a few trees in the back of the house. Diana had two hard ruddy fists, fooling around with the Eskimo pie in the lobby of The New Generation house, but they had stuck a dropper in both his eyes, so that it was impossible to tell who was starring and who was extra.

Joe made his way through the unfamiliar streets. A shower of debris fell from the window ledges. "Where's the x-ing?" queried a crippled girl in a pant suit. He didn't understand, shrugged, said, "I was gonna ask you. . ." She stared at him, like there was a meat grinder handle bolted to the side of his head.

Joe entered into a dark courtyard. "Hey kid, I'm looking for two old boys, Pakchaian—Lusik and Vsevolod. Heard of them?" The boy nearly fell off the balcony, "They're my two uncles!" "Shitting me?" "Fucked if I am." And the boy let drop a set of keys with a note, "Back soon, come up, make do—the kid is harmless, too."

The boy brought out a bottle of Courvoisier and poured out two shots earnestly. Then two more. Then they played last words.

"'More light'?"

"Edison?"

"Goethe. 'Get out'?"

"Marx."

"Right. Kant?"

"Don't know."

"'Good.' Abelard?"

"Don't know."

"Right."

Joe was beginning to get fuzzy. There was another round.

"Lusik used to be class president of sorts. . . Sevka, now, that's a whole other story. . ." said Joe.

Older versions of Lusik and Vsevolod came home and wanted to know about America. "America," said Joe, "America's all right. How are things here?" Lusik and Vsevolod were "in business": they had bought a house in Bastardov, kicked out the old folks and leased the first floor to a bank. But the bank folded and the first floor stood empty. That's half a mil in the outhouse. Suddenly Lusik remembered something and ran into the bedroom. He came back with a mug shaped like a bidet—it used to be Diana's favorite.

"How's old Lady Di?" inquired Vsevolod.

"Depends who you ask," said Joe. Three years ago Diana left him for a famous art-activist. He did a piece, lounging around a gallery, naked, in the company of several old-style alarm clocks, feeding on hot dogs. By way of grand finale he smeared himself with mustard and invited the public to lick him. Many resisted—Diana couldn't. The alarm clocks showed the exact times around the countries of the G8. Zemsic, or whatever his name, even got invited to the Belgrade biennale—he was that relevant.

"Ho!" said Joe, "I was headed for the graveyard."

"A bit early!" exclaimed Lusik and Vsevolod.

"I'm seeing Uncle Kotja."

Kotja was a shameless smoker, who lasted 96 years. His last words were, "Nobody should live this long," decided Joe for some reason. He found the gravestone beside the brick cemetery wall. The plot had been hijacked by bands of nettles; there was no one to look after it. Could ask the boy, thought Joe.

Foreigners equipped with floral arrangements wandered about the graveyard in search of kin, and Joe saw himself as a piece of a complex mechanism designed especially for nostalgic necro-nomads: here lies uncle, there is his daughter, here is first love, and over here is second love. He made a remark to this effect.

"Don't be so complicated, Jorka," retorted Lusik. (Vsevolod had stayed home to make dinner.)

"I'm trying," said Joe, catching sight of Diana Noyse.

Mountaineer Dr. Koch called his daughter "Devil's Barbie." 'Koch's alright, if you hold on tight' was a popular refrain on the slopes of the Elbrus. The old man was half-senile, but he could still do Vysotsky singalong at a peak picnic: "What could be better than mountains—mountains. . ." Baby Diana had golden ringlets—she screamed: I don't want the blue dress, I want the pink dress! And she got the pink dress every time. And what did he do? Climbed to the top of Coit Tower a year ago, called her from the payphone up there, shivering. Nothing. Why didn't she pick up? He did screw her periodically, didn't he? There was also a string of modest but genuine offerings. There were opera festivals in Verona and Salzburg. . .

"Diana?"

"Hey, Joe! Meet Zemsic. Zemsic—Joe."

A shaved head in chic goggles peeked out at him from behind the Koch monument.

*"Good to meet you, Joe. Cool place, huh?"* the head grinned.

"Zemsic wants to get an art intervention going here," explained Diana. "He says there's a real discourse potential."

"Right here?" asked Joe. "Cool."

"Why the hell did I waste five years of my life on that art-bag?" thought Joe, riding in the Pakchaian Lexus. "Could have married anybody. Back then it was easy. Everyone was somebody's cousin or best friend. Weekends at the dacha—spin the bottle—new dance every month."

"How's old Garik?" asked Joe. "He had a baby sister too—strip your soles, when you're not watching."

"Same as ever, huh? Well, what about his sister? Garik's in Moscow, he's "in business," like everyone else. Baby sister went to absolute shit." Lusik liked to wave his arms about. "The old girl borrowed a mil—at a very high rate. Her partner—also an American guy—he wasn't exactly versed in the ways of this world here—you know what I mean. . ."

Here something bumped them and threw them in the air, twisting them about and squeezing them into another dimension until a kind of truncated eternity came over them, held their skulls in a vise and crushed them, and all of a sudden a row of cages swayed in the heat of a summer afternoon, where the spectator and the exhibit are one and the same, and for a small fee you could have a handful of hay, observe (yourself) and scratch (yourself) roughly behind the ear, and stern-faced women are selling dusty melons by the entrance—they cut into them and extract a wondrous little pyramid, which they hold up toward you perched on the tips of their knives—try it, you'll like it, but there's no way you'll ever try it, you'll just get your lips cut to bloody bits.

It was pouring dreadfully at the funeral. Vsevolod pressed the boy close—the boy was sobbing; he kept saying, "two objects are identical not with respect to essences, but by virtue of their indifference. . ." Zemsic was shooting the funeral "in soft focus." His green sneakers flashed behind the dull gravestones. Diana hurried after him with an umbrella, hastily translating the basic points of the sermon and prayers. Discourse potential was swelling newly under his grasp.

*translated by Sergey Levchin*

# Nothing but Tights

They say he was jealous, but they also say some other things. They say he asked her to leave them on, and that she flat out refused, and so he went and strangled her—strangled her with tights!

Our neighbor's an American guy, but he's got a Russian surname, Ed Koslow, or maybe it's that they just never changed the name on the mailbox, because the super's an Aussi and he drinks, so I personally haven't seen him sober once, and I've been here two years almost. Koslow was an accountant and he did this heinous deed: strangulation, the woman practically his fiancée, with a pair of tights that she was wearing too. They found her in the kitchen, propped up against the fridge—she was already turning blue, tights around her neck, tongue all white sticking out—pretty picture.

I knew her. The crackpot had one every six months, but this one had been around for almost a year. He called her Chickadee, they say he proposed to her. Ever since I took a tumble on the steps and cracked my ankle I've had to use this cane going out, but mostly I just stay home—I see many things here, things I don't like, things I don't understand.

The following circumstances directly preceded and precipitated the crime. Koslow didn't approve of Chickadee's plans for the coming year, they included everything but Koslow, and she refused him, she said: I'll think it over, but she meant to cut it off (I got it from a client of his). Meaning, she might be up for it, every now and then at an inexpensive restaurant, where she doesn't have to know anyone, but these tights, for christ's sake, not in these tights, and his working away at her feet with his rough, callused hands (yes, he was an amateur gardener, sombrero on a stick, spraying avocados from a hose, we don't have avocados though, not like they do in Mexico, that's the truth) all oozing and buzzing, like it was a model beehive.

They met a year and a half ago, then lived a whole year together. It was through a mutual friend (she had killed her baby, that's a whole separate story)—realtor father was rolling in dough, and mother was a famous actress at one point, rising star of prime-time, as it were. But the rising star was long dead by then (cancer), though they did their best buying her doctors, and the dacha went for next to nothing—this was all back there still—the sister (not here) finished college, got hitched to a tennis player mad about music. But the hoarse patter not now, not now, you wild man, ever see that at Carnegie Hall? I don't think so. Country music in dead of winter, when the day drops like a firing squad, any old music, not just country, that's it—medicine for melancholia like tea with honey or better. Chickadee lost her confidence, but she'd lost interest even before that, he couldn't handle it, physically or emotionally. He went on loving her. He had a special lens attachment for his camera, then he switched to basic video equipment. Here she is on the steps going down to the beach, one leg swung over the other next to a fountain, a bubbly little thing, city fountain—people lived here before the war, then they were relocated, and the fountain was relocated, an exercise in futility; you wouldn't think it was the same city, that's how much it changed. It had to be renamed. She was smiling, drawing out her words. Weren't they long enough as it is? He said leave the tights on. She even asked about it: these come off? but she couldn't say tights, she just pointed, like it was a bad word or something. He nearly choked to death: don't you, don't do it, don't you dare. So she kept them on, then he kissed her fingers, and they were all full of rings. And the dark tights, but not black, just metallic brown with dark soles and a seam up the back, maybe.

She loved philosophizing, talking about Bergson and Paul Ricoeur, he just nodded and said nothing, didn't want her to see the gaps. He had some—gaps, that is. Big ones. Sure he loved reading, but philosophy, you can just forget it. Too bad, though, philosophy and literature are one and the same (there's any number of things we could say to the world, but the world—it's always one and the same—the world doesn't talk back), there aren't any protagonists-antagonists in philosophy, otherwise it's the same as literature, with ideas in place of characters: ideas unfolding where events should be, zooming in on ideas not landscapes, because nowadays nobody's gonna care about ooh a landscape, nobody's gonna be chasing you around for a story. Maybe the idiots will. But we get stories bright and early with our coffee, thanks to journals and journalists, and the papers had at least a hundred dead at a Bronx disco fire, seems like disasters all around. Some kid got half his skull blown off with a shell, they had to graft it by way of a special process, took a month just to get the ear to stick in the right place. Or a maid from Burma got her nose chewed off and some lips. Instead we have ideas: essences, perceptions, apperceptions. He'd asked a whole bunch of them, before this Chickadee came along, he'd asked them to leave the tights on, some did and some didn't, but most did. He took one to the movies, he was just a kid then, and there in the movie house he was stroking her tights, and that's when it started, since then he'd had this kind of special interest. I don't want to get too graphic here, but when he asked a lady (this was a sort of fetish for him) to keep her tights on, with his whole hands and his fingers, first his rough, callused fingers, he didn't want the lady, object of desire, to slip off her stockings, everything comes off, but that. Before this one (and before her killer girlfriend), when he had another one coming over from Venezuela and they drank together, they really got tight on tequila (Mockingbird brand), though he could tell she was faking, making like she was more drunk than she was, so she didn't have to feel so ashamed taking off her pants. He woke up around seven and there she was, pouting in her sleep, right up into his shoulder, he wanted to take her then and there, like having a dead body but still warm, and living and with tights on, but she'd managed to slip them off somehow, he didn't even notice, and so he didn't take her, just felt her a little there, where they have tights and other things, typically. Bras, brastraps, he flipped up her dress (killer girlfriend was hiding out on a dacha outside of Moscow, where they had property, he brought her cigarettes from the States in the early days when the reforms put the kibosh on everything, smokes included, they were rolling wallpaper, shredding tights, and rolling them in wallpaper and that's what they smoked—"smoked" in quotation marks—more like choked on, like those patients at a TB clinic, Proletariat blvd. (they also faked it), when, let's say, this is pure conjecture, the nurse came calling in white tights, she's not staying, you see, making like she's just there for a minute, she'd meant to call next door, but the minute turned into leap year, they would see each other, and he never once had to ask her to leave them on, she saw everything with her own eyes and she left them on. Fishnets, like the ones she used to wear, that handsome zoology instructor, and he loved to watch her through the dog's skeleton! Through the crack of the greyhound's ribs. The crisscross of the tights through that crack (sister tossed the baby all by herself, smashed its ribs, death came, then husband came, she's already a mental case, shaking all over, crossing herself and cussing, that's why she was hiding out at the dacha, they did a nationwide manhunt, looked for her everywhere and they found her, got a warrant out for her arrest, but they couldn't prove anything: where's the baby? gone, maybe stolen). It was her word against her husband's, and he'd been out of work for over a year then, the management at the factory where they also made nylons, incidentally, didn't exactly give him a stellar review. So she'd lost all faith in him. Didn't love him anymore. He wasn't ready for it, he just went on buying her shoes, one size too big, that was his thing. He loved to touch her feet and sniff them through the opening in a kind of foot harness they make. She was giggling: it tickles, like that was his business; tickles, just shut up and deal with it, for chirst's sake.

It drove her crazy, his manias, his pathological phobias. Even the lamest of parties, a crumpled evening that you just wanted to throw away and never think about as long as you lived—even that was subject to exhaustive analysis, performed over break-fast the next morning, of who said what, and looked where, and moved what, doesn't matter if it had nothing or anything to do with him. Like Ninka, she's the one that did the robot the other night. They were all begging her: Ninka, do the robot, you know you want to. Ninka made like she didn't want to, for appearances' sake, but then she went and whoa! she did the robot. Man, she did the robot, first she did the robot backwards, then she did the robot forwards. She did it strokin' robot, she did it smokin' robot, slam robot, spam robot, and then she did the robot roll. Dumbass robot? Yessir! Apeshit robot? Yesma'am! Dada robot—yes indeed, and then she did the robot roll. This robot went to Hollywood, and that robot went to Bollywood, robot's looking for his shoe, and the rabbi robot too. Hey, my old lady goes hungry, scarfing hotdogs in a tree! Hey-ho, robot, here we go! Man on woman, do the robot, on my bonny, do the robot, and on your bonny do the robot, hey-ho robot, here we go! Everybody's doin' it—sweaty robot, doin' it, natty robot, doin' it, batty robot doin' it! Stroke of midnight, do the robot, crack o'mornin' do the robot, 8:07 do the robot, hit the barracks, do the robot. But my old lady, she goes hungry, scarfing hotdogs in a tree. Bigger robot, better robot, best of all possible robots. Hey robot, ho robot, brave new stinkin' robot.

*translated by Sergey Levchin*

# Once in a Lifetime

## 1

One time, an acquaintance of mine, a gossip monger slash drummer in the post-feminist art collective Attaboy informed me, in a theatrical whisper, at the lawyer John O'Reilly's 40th birthday bash, that Kosta's great-grandmother was the very same half-Greek Miss whom Ivan Alexeyevich Bunin had been married to in his youth. I don't know. I simply can't imagine where this pretty airhead, all falling out of her décolletage at the sight of the least bit pulled together bachelor (and I'm not just talking about myself here, but also about John, even though he's married to the charming Dorothy P., as well as about Kosta himself), could have obtained such privy intelligence. And indeed, how is it possible, that among the descendants of an Odessan dame, Anna Tsakni, subsequently de Ribas, would appear such a great-grandson as Kosta, a 100% unalloyed Greek by the way and, to boot, who owns (or rather, owned) a newsstand on the corner of Houston and Thompson, not far from the location of my favorite Tibetan restaurant?

## 2

An older brother sent his younger brother money for a ticket, telling him at once to come to America; their father didn't want to leave, so the brother went by himself. The American brother didn't really want the father to come anyway: they didn't get along, the father had a bit of a temper, a heavy hand, and a pronounced trachoma; a trachoma then was grounds for refusal in America. So that when the father said: "I'm not going anywhere; it's too late for me to begin my life anew," the older brother was not particularly saddened. The younger brother, Isak, spoke almost not a word of American, only Good-may, good-may, something a nutty socialist from Vinnitsa had taught him on the ship, which means: Good day, my brother workers, best wishes to you for our upcoming little spring holiday!

And so their ship is mooring at the pier, a fine mist rain is falling, and the buildings are all so incredibly high, he had never seen anything like them before, what would they be doing in their shtetl? But what amazed him even more than the height of the buildings was the number of Jews on the ship, and especially ashore—Romanian, Polish, all sorts, etcetera etcetera. He even thought at first that he had landed in that ancient kingdom that his grandfather, the one that didn't return from the Russian-Japanese War, had told him about in his fairy tales.

## 3

From here on out, we will hear in exhaustive detail about various elements of day-to-day life; after all, I don't live in a vacuum, but down the hall, and to the right. But still, I'd like to make this a bit more radical, more intricate; the familiar, that's for later, for sweet memories: well, let's just say he's a good man, absolutely adores children, but took to alcohol and, as a result, let himself go completely, yes, a total waste, so that even his friends and family turned away from him—it's as clear as day, no need for explications: depression sets in, or the girlfriend leaves him for another woman. But let's say he's a dedicated family man, but is having an affair with the neighbor's Saint Bernard, coddling him with expensive presents (bought an elegant muzzle from Cartier for Christmas, an 85%-fine silver leash from Tiffany's for National Four-footed Friend Day), now that's already out of the ordinary and demands an explanation. In other words, extraordinary circumstances, asocial personalities, novel psychogeographical land-scapes require more precise details and in-depth considerations of motives. Etc. "I kiss you, I love you, forever, your sweet little sausage," every Dick, Jane, and Harry understands that, but "Hate you, kill that bitch," signed "your demon seed" calls for some elabo-ration or, as a certain Moscow cellist, a regular at the Slavic Bazaar restaurant, had once, if not quite tastefully, very vividly expressed it: mmm, this here *lyulya-kebob* gots to be chewed on rea-al good now, my young darlings, so go ahead and get to them juicy bits.

4

**P**oor Kosta! When he was found, all his feathers ruffled and he half-naked, in Coney Island, squashed behind the door of a phone booth, with that awful six ft. section of pipe in his clenched teeth and birdlike glassy eyes, the cries of the beach vendors, "Buy your cotton candy here! Ice cold beer! Ice cold beer!" were indeed coming from here and not from there, where his soul was, at that very moment, departing. A woman snake with a girl lizard found him on their lunch break. The snake wearing an emerald colored body glove was in the act of opening the phone booth door, focused on sliding a hot quarter into the slot to call her medical assistant husband's pager, so as to dis-cuss with him the details of their forthcoming pleasure cruise up the Hudson when the little lizard began chattering: "Ma, get a load of this! They wacked the clown!" The snake, so stunned by what she saw, especially the dead man's nose and wig, that she almost choked on her sandwich, made the call—to the precinct of course, not the husband. In a split second, they wrote out the report: snake, witnesses, etc. . . The lizard even forgot about her Nintendo, whimpered the entire day Saturday, couldn't fall asleep. Six years old, they're quite impressionable at that age. (Kosta didn't have any children: "I don't want to take on the re-

sponsibility for another life in this world, one that inspires neither confidence nor optimism." His own words.)

## 5

The main thing here is to immediately and without further delay declare: are they or are they not animals? This is what we
have to get straight: are they arsonists, rioters, agitators, lusting
after the possessions of others, or are other people's things truly,
as their social geneticist professors insist, long-forgotten objects
that had once belonged to them. Are they Luddites, bandits, as
per the narco-baron millions slinging powdery sand into the well-
oiled and noiseless, even though often idle, working mechanism
of the government machinery. Your and my bureaucracy, ladies
and gentlemen, my fellow taxpayers. The wet nurse of our fore-
fathers, who had squirted, and continues to squirt, from the teats
of justice and lawfulness into the mouths of those babes, Romulus
and Remus, or have you forgotten your history? Who the heck's
E. Gibbon, you say? Wreckers of our nests, and not just in parallel
reality, but right here, right here under our noses! Immediately
cease and desist from your virulent sabotage, you half-breeds!

Who are you anyway? You are invisible on the network news,
on Fox and CNN, you're not heard on the radio. You're not out
promenading your poodles while giving a tongue-lashing to your
succubi boyfriends over your handheld devices. You're hidden
from our gazes, just like the juvenile mushrooms between the toes
of the overworked cleaning lady, pani Milena, who is temporar-
ily ensconced at her sister-in-law's in Williamsburg; the groceries
are cheaper there, and it's easier getting by without knowing the
language. May you be damned, then! You miserable idiots!

Thus: she licketh the balls of their headman, verily, lickety-
split to a billiard-like shine, the pretty girl, flexible of limb and
hollow of bone. Thereaft, they saddled her, and putteth her to the

scourge. She moaned, but meeklier, so that they were not a-com-ing, but withheld their seed. He covered her pubis with a ritual pubic kerchief, hand-knitted and netlike that the Hilina woman smuggled out of Oslo at the risk to her life along with the other valuables. Then, they setteth its edges on fire. She wailed out of fear, even louder than before, more forcibly than previous. Then, carefully, they encumbered upon her mouth-cav with many a member. Her sword-swallower brother forbade them from giv-ing things their natural name, rebuked them for that either/or. As in ire. They gave their best shot then, not leaning on all oars, rather gobbling up an anemic omelet made of broken whites only, taking the rap for everyone: boy was it hot.

This is what happened next: who, lustily, for the sheer pleasure of it, and in a premeditated way deprived her of life: well? Kolchak himself. Or more precisely—mom's idiot-maimer. After all, she's got beautiful heels, hidden in the recesses of each a moist, warm place, but loosey-goosey and without the sharp teeth, the inci-sors. This isn't some fantasy, I tell you, I saw it myself, there are witnesses. It's straight out of this moronic life. I wasn't brought up to invent such things. I write from nature, but more colorfully than it is in reality, with compositional excesses and telling it all aslant, and then also to be able to sell it to the market. I write so that you may be able to live easier afterward, when neither I nor death any longer (almost) exist. But then again, go ahead, live as you know best, you lotus eaters. It's coming soon. Sooner even than it was in the past (speaking hypothetically).

## 6

What do I know about Kosta?
Kosta liked to drink. Drink a lot. By the time the Italians would peek into the restaurant, Kosta would already be tipsy. Laia was busting his balls, trying not to give him any—all for

nothing. His mustache smelled of wine, and the suntan attracted the youngest of female admirers. From behind the gauze, which for the third year now served as their curtain, Laia had watched everything. The purple phallus of the cell phone in the hands of the fat-breasted Monica from Naples, quivering as she was from exhaustion, and Kosta self-importantly showing off to her the previous autumn's tourist attractions.

"Minareto," Kosta would say with a note of squeamishness in his voice. Laia didn't feel any jealousy. Zen, years of meditation, yoga on the mat. Whom should she be jealous of? The two-week dabblers seeking a transitory feeling of completeness at their lodge? Or was it for tiny, swarthy-faced Barbara who, judging by the avalanche of tampons in the bathroom, was in a permanent state of ovulation.

Kosta wore a hat throughout the summer. Monica would laugh: Kosta, your head needs to breathe. It's got pores. Kosta would only snort in response. He didn't understand in Italian.

One time Monica accidentally dropped Kosta's purple cell phone on the floor. Its glass screen cracked. Kosta's countenance turned dark, he got off Monica and poured himself a glass of wine. "Quanto costa, stupido?"—the fair-headed co-ed queried. Meaning, don't have a cow, I'll buy you a new one, why don't you notice instead how moist and swell I am. But he was a stubborn, hot-headed Greek, from a diminutive touristy village where even the asses have the backsides of professional bicycle riders.

Of course, Laia saw everything from behind the gauze curtain, but she wasn't jealous. Toward whom? The Neapolitan simpleton who, judging by the layer of wet wool at low tide in the bathtub, was suffering from catastrophic hair loss? The he-goat would get over it after the rutting season was over.

## 7

When the Germans would come into the restaurant, they would order dishes whose names they couldn't pronounce. What paklafa?

Barbara got a job for the summer washing dishes in the neighboring village. She had a friendly, open face and several gold teeth, in which the Aegean Sea was reflected and piddly mountains deprived of all vegetation, the billowing gauze and Kosta's cell phone, now no longer purple but a sun-bleached maroon, left him by Monica in memory of their summer vacation. However, how long can you continue living on memories until you're found out and judged ripe to be jumped from behind.

She liked the smell of Kosta's wine, liked his unfocused gaze, the thick hair on his belly and chest. She must have been an Albanian. Oh-oh, she sighed with her entire heaving chest, when Kosta decided to give her a shellacking during the lunch break in the employee's room. He was quite goal-oriented with her, and she ... well she couldn't ... or perhaps could ... you know, it's difficult to say now, with any degree of certainty.

And so Kosta took her away to warmer climes.

Laia didn't even have time to feel surprised when Kosta told her: it's over, Laia. She began trembling: how dare you, am I some sort of tart to you—slapping my face like it's some gauntlet in the face of fortune. Her Zen had slackened that day. She rode a motorcycle into town, didn't slow down coming into a curve, and crashed among the hills winding in the darkness.

The flat roofs of the white two-story houses, a rectangle of blue sky—the view from the hospital window. Only in August did she return to her native Hoboken, New Jersey. And you know her parents had warned her all along: think about it well, Laia. Your entire life is ahead of you, dear girl. And the issue here isn't that he's Greek and older, but that he's a Greek and a souse.

## 8

Once again, the blue, cloudless sky, but now in a completely different country. The silver, rented Renault, nature, gas pumps, pines on precipitous cliffs, some or other escarpment, more likely Spain than Italy, probably Alicante and not Malaga, road signs in an incomprehensible language... Their stomachs ached, all the digestive juices conscripted into metabolizing the unfamiliar food. Barbara was smacking her lips, fidgeting around first this way then that, ignoring the rules of proper behavior in the passenger seat. They'd talked about it before, and more than once: "We'll get to the hotel, and do it..." But they've got to have it right now, they've got an itch they can't get to scratch enough.

Although it should be said that love had taken the back seat for Kosta already some five years ago, when that drunk Swedish girl Nicole scalded him from a pitcher, during their tryst in the sauna. He was no longer insanely drawn to all the immigrant Haitian girls, it wasn't constantly on his mind as it was that July when he, as a seventeen-year-old, walked across Stigmata Square toward the Museum of Aviation, while in his mind he was screwing anything and everything that moved: the young ones, the very young ones, the not so young, even the lame ones. Now, it's different: three bitches—one near at hand, Barbara with her tattoos in the most unimaginable places, and the two lesbos in the back (Khlashka and Lotta) were just part of the landscape, though truth be told of a transitory landscape. A movable feast, as it were, that's a part of them, that's always with them. Yes, that's right: vaginas. Just like that: squat, grunt, strain, and pop them right out. But so what? Badgers have vaginas too, and quails give birth, to eggs that is. So what's the tsimis, the populi? So that everything around doesn't just croak, is that the point? Is that what rocks your boat, having things around? Not so much? 4000 years of shit, but let's hope that in a year or two everything will change, and only for the better? We'll restore the ozone layer, permanently freeze the glaciers so that they don't melt where they're not supposed to. Bullshit, things will change, bullshit, we'll restore everything. Then why bother working your ass off for a paying customer, my fellow passengers, why bother getting an eyeful of the badly washed asses of the opposite sex, constantly lusting after them, all for the sake of being alive in another 100 years, amid exactly the same shit, but now under a different name, and with different shows to watch on the telly?

9

"Let us consider the following for a minute: what is time."
"Say what?!"

"What is time, essentially? The category of time. The substance of time. Let's reason this out."

"What are you talking about? What 'reason it out?' Since when are you a philosopher?"

"OK, but still, really—what is time?"

"Time is when the guests have arrived but you're still not there. And they are waiting at the door, but no one is answering. They ring the bell repeatedly, getting irritated, already wanting to leave, they had bought the wine for nothing. But then you arrive. Make a hundred apologies, you'd run out to get a pack of smokes. And you, overjoyed, flushed, your coat flung open, hatless, this October that has fallen on us a cold one—and one of the guests, her name is Ronnie, suspects that you have a new girlfriend, but Ronnie doesn't have a clue that your new girlfriend is none other than her best friend. And there's a multitude of guests, and food also: both goose pâté and vegetarian. Three bottles of champagne! And so, hesitatingly, you take it upon yourself to pose a question. Who's responsible for everything that is around us, who is in charge of the universe, of all creation, of this colossal structure; it couldn't possibly be left to fend for itself. Who is it that promenades all those beautiful girls on the embankment? Model-thin and shapely, and whom you have an urge to follow and, once you've caught up and are even with them, to tell them something uncommonly inventive? In answer, total silence. Not worthy of reply. And when the tourist fell of his motorcycle going at a modest speed, but still broke his arm, his model-thin, shapely girlfriend (Ronnie) betrayed him (virtually) with the manager of the internet café. And this made him lose it completely, and for quite a while. And he composed a futuristic story, which began like this: It is dripping out of the sky's ass; the dick-sun no longer burns the skin with its smegma of rays. In some sense, Ronnie is being sliced up by a dick, Ronnie's giggling, all covered with blood, ditsy Ronnie's having her teeth knocked out with dirty boots. Screaming, is she? I want some more, give it to me! Ronnie's already passing out from being (that is what time is, you bastards!) ravaged. I'm seeing you here for the first time; likewise—neither you mine, nor I his—dare question my motives, or her plans, not a thing. Silence. The devil's own amalgam of cruelty and sensuality. In the human zoo of irrevocable political and social utopias (whether you vote or don't vote, what you get, anyway, is bubkes) the father uses the son as a surrogate for a hidden camera. An absolutely once-in-a-lifetime occurrence."

## 10

Who are these people, running around nameless, without a biography? People whose lives are inconsequential to us, whose death will in no way become part of our tragedy. These crowds in the metro stations, these squawking youth—you can't even thread your way to the bar to order a drink—exchanging banal double entendres. Wailing away like their great-grandfathers, those that didn't come back from the Great War, their late great-grandmothers, puffing away on their last Chesterfield cigarettes, provocatively staring directly into the eyes of the heroes in military uniforms. And squawking. When will we too get to dance that newfangled "Fox-trot," and when will they start writing it without the hyphen and the quotation marks, when, Harry?

Well, Harry?

But Harry remains silent.

Your Harry's still in the fox hole, with his gas mask on. Harry's no more, grandma. Your Harry didn't make it home from the war.

## 11

During one of those October days when no one wants to think about the rains, but only about the summer, that was only just here but now is gone, and the leaves—like they have a mind of their own, the leaves flit about everywhere and crumble under the heels of the youth raising a racket, some bullshit about Kosta Devyatkos having been slammed in the news rag. Kosta Devyatkos! From the history department! Of all the people! For what, did you say? Debauchery? No way, have you ever heard of such a thing? What debauchery? Besides female forms—and by the way quite stylized ones, those in the lousy reproduction of the bas-relief from the era of pharaoh Shishak, and the two-three statues of the royal ladies of the Eighteenth Dynasty—he never even laid an eye on the opposite sex. Perhaps just once, in his third year, he had ogled Bella-Barbarella—and that only briefly. The girls from the laboratory—not a dram of attention, even though they were pointy of breast and curvaceous of thigh. Not even when Nastya Pelipenko, just for the sake of conducting an experiment, handed him her panties wrapped in a newspaper to sniff at; and the schmuck blurts out: "Chopped chuck. No, not chopped chuck. I take my words back. Not chuck, shellac. I know: my little sister dabbles with paints." You see, it's just not his thing. Why keep hassling the guy? Let the poor buy be.

## 12

Obituary: the face is the same, but the name isn't. The photograph however clearly matches. Although, besides a name, people have a biography. An obituary in the Russian paper, and one in the American also. But the two disagree. An accident, but in the Russian version there's no mention of it. It says: died unexpectedly. Three obituaries: the husband's, the husband's family, and somebody else's. Parents in Moscow. Friends. She worked part-time as a model (a human manikin). But in reality. . .

You can never return to the same city.

He was driving to the funeral of his former wife and remembered how they had become acquainted, episodes from her childhood, how she was unfaithful to him, how much sorrow and distress she had caused him. How he beat her full force. . . Lots of things happened. In the town of Arles, he did the girl doggie style, with a view of Van Gogh's poppies. Dry the pussy was, unreceptive. But he did her anyway.

Is that really her in the coffin? Looks like her. Looks like? Well, in a coffin everyone looks a bit different. They had watched *Last Tango* together. The part where the husband delivers a monologue at his wife's coffin. And so the end result is that, even though they had lived together fighting like cats and dogs, still, no one else ever came along who was dearer to him than she had been.

## 13

Grandfather had dreamed of America, but didn't go, it didn't work out, another hadn't even dreamed about it but went and things also didn't work out, and someone else dreamed and went, and everything happened for him, but who was that, anyway? And why doesn't he reply to anyone's letters? Because he works all the time, that's why. And aunt Esther works all the time but still answers her letters, and writes to her brother in a large script without almost a single blemish:

"You think that the fireflies in Pennsylvania are sparks, flying from under the car hood. And you keep turning over in your head: The last thing we need right now is to get stuck. On the highway, at night.

And only approaching Chicago do you understand that you are being followed. A former friend? But a former friend—is an enemy. Armed and dangerous. Or just a simpleton. And therefore also dangerous?

And the actual sparks from under the hood appeared only once we got to Nevada. And soon after, clouds of white smoke. We barely hissed and wobbled our way into the body shop in Sacramento."

## 14

And in conclusion, in the space of three pages—about her misadventures, about how they barely reached the port at Little Peapod on a horse-drawn cart, and how in Hamburg they had wanted to remove her and the child from the steamer, where they had slept on barrels of herring from Holland, and how they were then almost sent back from Ellis Island because Moishe was taken sick en route, his nose dripping God knows what, and how she was looking her husband over once they were on shore and thinking: could he have changed so much in these past three years; and he had indeed changed, and besides, he hadn't showed up, staying to work the second shift at the women's clothing store owned by some Perkel guy, where he was boxing underwear and bras; there was a genuine boom in the sales of these at the time, the suffragettes had dropped their corsets and had nothing to wear to work, acceleration of production, Taylorism, narrative retardation, but also an invitation to a journey—there are still plenty of empty seats available, ladies and gentlemen.

*translated by Alex Cigale*

# Cat–Dogs

"Not cat-dogs, hot dogs. That's sausages with ketchup and sauerkraut to you. They are sold here on every street corner. There's no such thing as cat-dogs."

"Yes, I know. I have a friend in Chicago, a millionaire."

"No kidding!"

"Oh no!"

"So how did he get rich, your friend?"

"In the simplest way. He inherited capital."

"And he didn't put it to work, so to speak compounded the interest?"

"Perhaps he did, how should I know? You think he shares everything with me?"

"And what did his father, Papa Faza, make his money on?"

"He started out by delivering a pizza. It went well so he delivered another. Then he hired a bunch of cucarachas, that's what they call pizza delivery boys here. Now they make the deliveries. Then he launched his own pizzeria. And then another. And then another again."

"And what's your trade?"

"I'm writing a story about uncle Shlava Baedeker."

"This is your main line of work?"

"That's the case for now."

"They pay you well?"

"I'm not complaining."

"What kind of a name is that, Shlava?"

"Nickname. Everyone called him Slava, but he had a speech impediment and would insert consonants in all sorts of places."

"And so, what's it about, your fiction?"

"Two people go off to mother Russia, to make some money. One of them disappears, and the other searches for him."

"And does he find him?"

"Finds him, he does. But he would've been better off not looking. It was one big rigmarole..."

... a fragment of a conversation between two passengers at a bus stop, in a Greek town on the shores of the Aegean Sea. The time: 9:52 am. A bus with a sign reading Plotin (sic) was running late. A group of students had placed a package of beer in a plastic bag in a puddle to keep it cold. It was getting hot.

... he first went with women. Then he understood that with men, it's easier, and the pleasure is about the same.

You spend 10 years in school. You start out a pure, little, round-faced boy. You end up an emaciated onanist with sideburns and an unhealthy complexion.

"Ergo?"

"Endo, not ergo: if one only knew these things in advance."

And yet another plot, an alternative, as it were, a remake of Oedipus Rex but without the cursing. The soothsayer predicts that uncle Shlava will die at the hands of his son. Uncle Shlava drops everything, his family included, and goes to America. Endo, you think?

Uncle Shlava Baedeker, a bony man with the face of a salamander, but attractive in a manly way, even though entirely browless, went on vacation every September. Returning in middle of October, he promenaded the city streets in his proud, sun-baked solitude. And in May, he helped us migrate to our summer dacha. One time, near some tramcar tracks, he put his car in reverse and smacked into some dumbass in a Moskvich automobile, and the guy jumps out of his vehicle and was about to tear the key out of the ignition, but Uncle Shlava wrestles for the keys with him and, finit. And that's how I'd like him to be remembered: in his Zhiguli car, with his tensing jowls and his clenched teeth, or across the street from the Army Surplus store with his lively howl of "Anyone for ice cream?": I don't think I had time to mention it, that Uncle Shlava was an ice cream man.

The very same one about whom the late multimedia artist, Karen Springs from Naxos, did a project, the same one who rewrote a text taking into account the Greek context; it was easier that way to score a grant for it:

The Greek ice cream man shutters his stand for the winter, when he makes ends meet as a taxi driver in Athens. And so his flight lands, he catches a cab, and his colleague recognizes him, another ice cream man, or a barber. The island's normally full of tourists. And the man refuses to accept payment for the trip. They almost come to blows, but then take off to knock down a glass of ouzo together, on the Stigmata Square and. . . I don't want to go on. I don't want to record it all down, to pretend like I'm Karen Springs, I don't want to, and I don't have to. Karen Springs, and who the hell is this Springs? The one that springs for the money, that pulls the purse strings.

On the island, the need for an interlocutor became progressively less vital, and the need to compare a mosquito keeping me awake at night to a motorcyclist without a sidecar, a driver's license, or helmet, but with a long proboscis and a thirst for every drop of my hot blood—vice versa.

Do you know me? That is, did you know me? Remember me? That is, have you come to remember me? I've managed to spread the scent mark of my individuality, but did I also display an awareness of the tradition? Did I manage to shake all of you up, falling asleep at the computer screen? Seduce the woman in the orange summer dress from the laundromat? Yes, yes, no, yes, no, yes.

*translated by Alex Cigale*

Made in the USA
Middletown, DE
18 December 2020